He was a fully grown man, alone in a dense forest, with no trail to show where he had come from and no memory to tell who—or what he was.

His eyes were not human eyes.

The forest people took him in and raised him almost as a child, teaching him to speak, training him in forest lore, giving him all the knowledge they had. But they could not solve the riddle of his past, and at last he had to set out on a quest to Es Toch, the City of the Shing, the Liars of Earth, the Enemy of Mankind.

There he would find out the truth about himself . . . and a universe of danger.

URSULA KROEBER LE GUIN, daughter of A. L. Kroeber (anthropologist) and Theodora Kroeber (author), was born in Berkeley, California in 1929. She attended college at Radcliffe and Columbia, and married C. A. LeGuin in Paris in 1951. The LeGuins and their three children live in Portland, Oregon.

Ursula LeGuin's novels include ROCANNON'S WORLD, PLANET OF EXILE, CITY OF ILLUSIONS and THE LEFT HAND OF DARKNESS, all published by Ace Books. THE LEFT HAND OF DARKNESS in particular attracted wide attention and strong praise; it was awarded both the Nebula and the Hugo Awards.

CITY OF ILLUSIONS

URSULA K. LeGUIN

SF
ace books
A Division of Charter Communications Inc.
A GROSSET & DUNLAP COMPANY
51 Madison Avenue
New York, New York 10010

CITY OF ILLUSIONS

This Printing: November 1980
Published simultaneously in Canada

8 0 9
Manufactured in the United States of America

IMAGINE DARKNESS.

In the darkness that faces outward from the sun a mute spirit woke. Wholly involved in chaos, he knew no pattern. He had no language, and did not know the darkness to be night.

As unremembered light brightened about him he moved, crawling, running sometimes on all fours, sometimes pulling himself erect, but not going anywhere. He had no way through the world in which he was, for a way implies a beginning and an end. All things about him were tangled, all things resisted him. The confusion of his being was impelled to movement by forces for which he knew no name: terror, hunger, thirst, pain. Through the dark forest of things he blundered in silence till the night stopped him, a greater force. But when the light began again he groped on. When he broke out into the sudden broad sunlight of the Clearing he rose upright and stood a moment. Then he put his hands over his eyes and cried out aloud.

Weaving at her loom in the sunlit garden, Parth saw him at the forest's edge. She called to the others with a quick beat of her mind. But she feared nothing, and by the time the others came out of the house she had gone across the Clearing to the uncouth figure that crouched among the high, ripe grasses. As they approached they saw her put her hand on his shoulder and bend down to him, speaking softly.

She turned to them with a wondering look, saying, "Do you see his eyes . . .?"

They were strange eyes, surely. The pupil was large; the iris, of a grayed amber color, was oval lengthwise so that the white of the eye did not show at all. "Like a cat," said Garra. "Like an egg all yolk," said Kai, voicing the slight distaste of uneasiness roused by that small, essential difference. Otherwise the stranger seemed only a man, under the mud and scratches and filth he had got over his face and naked body in his aimless struggle through the forest; at most he was a little paler-skinned than the brown people who now surrounded him, discussing him quietly as he crouched in the sunlight, cowering and shaking with exhaustion and fear.

Though Parth looked straight into his strange eyes no spark of human recognition met her there. He was deaf to their speech, and did not understand their gestures.

"Mindless or out of his mind," said Zove. "But also starving; we can remedy that." At this Kai and young Thurro half led half dragged the shambling fellow into the house. There they and Parth and Buckeye managed to feed and clean him, and got him onto a pallet, with a shot of sleep-dope in his veins to keep him there.

"Is he a Shing?" Parth asked her father.

"Are you? Am I? Don't be naive, my dear," Zove answered. "If I could answer that question I could set Earth free. However, I hope to find out if he's mad or sane or

2

imbecile, and where he came from, and how he came by those yellow eyes. Have men taken to breeding with cats and falcons in humanity's degenerate old age? Ask Kretyan to come up to the sleeping-porches, daughter."

Parth followed her blind cousin Kretyan up the stairs to the shady, breezy balcony where the stranger slept. Zove and his sister Karell, called Buckeye, were waiting there. Both sat cross-legged and straight-backed, Buckeye playing with her patterning frame, Zove doing nothing at all: a brother and sister getting on in years, their broad, brown faces alert and very tranquil. The girls sat down near them without breaking the easy silence. Parth was a reddish-brown color with a flood of long, bright, black hair. She wore nothing but a pair of loose silvery breeches. Kretyan, a little older, was dark and frail; a red band covered her empty eyes and held her thick hair back. Like her mother she wore a tunic of delicately woven figured cloth. It was hot. Midsummer afternoon burned on the gardens below the balcony and out on the rolling fields of the Clearing. On every side, so close to this wing of the house as to shadow it with branches full of leaves and wings, so far in other directions as to be blued and hazed by distance, the forest surrounded them.

The four people sat still for quite a while, together and separate, unspeaking but linked. "The amber bead keeps slithering off into the Vastness pattern," Buckeye said with a smile, setting down her frame with its jewel-strung, crossing wires.

"All your beads end up in Vastness," her brother said. "An effect of your suppressed mysticism. You'll end up like our mother, see if you don't, able to see the patterns on an empty frame."

3

"Suppressed fiddledof fiddle," Buckeye remarked. "I never suppressed anything in my life."

"Kretyan," said Zove, "the man's eyelids move. He may be in a dreaming cycle."

The blind girl moved closer to the pallet. She reached out her hand, and Zove guided it gently to the stranger's forehead. They were all silent again. All listened. But only Kretyan could hear.

She lifted her bowed, blind head at last.

"Nothing," she said, her voice a little strained.

"Nothing?"

"A jumble—a void. He has no mind."

"Kretyan, let me tell you how he looks. His feet have walked, his hands have worked. Sleep and the drug relax his face, but only a thinking mind could use and wear a face into these lines."

"How did he look when he was awake?"

"Afraid," said Parth. "Afraid, bewildered."

"He may be an alien," Zove said, "not a Terran man, though how that could be— But he may think differently than we. Try once more, while he still dreams."

"I'll try, uncle. But I have no sense of any mind, of any true emotion or direction. A baby's mind is frightening but this . . . is worse—darkness and a kind of empty jumble—"

"Well, then keep out," Zove said easily. "No-mind is an evil place for mind to stay."

"His darkness is worse than mine," said the girl. "This is a ring, on his hand. . . ." She had laid her hand a moment on the man's, in pity or as if asking his unconscious pardon for her eavesdropping on his dreams.

"Yes, a gold ring without marking or design. It was all he wore on his body. And his mind stripped naked as his flesh. So the poor brute comes to us out of the forest—sent by whom?"

All the family of Zove's House except the little children gathered that night in the great hall downstairs, where high windows stood open to the moist night air. Starlight and the presence of trees and the sound of the brook all entered into the dimly lit room, so that between each person and the next, and between the words they said, there was a certain space for shadows, night-wind, and silence.

"Truth, as ever, avoids the Stranger," the Master of the House said to them in his deep voice. "This stranger brings us a choice of several unlikelihoods. He may be an idiot born, who blundered here by chance; but then, who lost him? He may be a man whose brain has been damaged by accident, or tampered with by intent. Or he may be a Shing masking his mind behind a seeming amentia. Or he may be neither man nor Shing; but then, what is he? There's no proof or disproof for any of these notions. What shall we do with him?"

"See if he can be taught," said Zove's wife Rossa.

The Master's eldest son Metock spoke: "If he can be taught, then he is to be distrusted. He may have been sent here to be taught, to learn our ways, insights, secrets. The cat brought up by the kindly mice."

"I am not a kindly mouse, my son," the Master said.

"Then you think him a Shing?"

"Or their tool."

"We're all tools of the Shing. What would you do with him?"

"Kill him before he wakes."

The wind blew faintly, a whippoorwill called out in the humid, starlit Clearing.

5

"I wonder," said the Oldest Woman, "if he might be a victim, not a tool. Perhaps the Shing destroyed his mind as punishment for something he did or thought. Should we then finish their punishment?"

"It would be truer mercy," Metock said.

"Death is a false mercy," the Oldest Woman said bitterly.

So they discussed the matter back and forth for some while, equably but with a gravity that included both moral concern and a heavier, more anxious care, never stated but only hinted at whenever one of them spoke the word *Shing*. Parth took no part in the discussion, being only fifteen, but she listened intently. She was bound by sympathy to the stranger and wanted him to live.

Rayna and Kretyan joined the group; Rayna had been running what physiological tests she could on the stranger, with Kretyan standing by to catch any mental response. They had little to report as yet, other than that the stranger's nervous system and the sense areas and basic motor capacity of his brain seemed normal, though his physical responses and motor skill compared with those of a year-old child, perhaps, and no stimulus of localities in the speech area had got any response at all. "A man's strength, a baby's coordination, an empty mind," Ranya said.

"If we don't kill him like a wild beast," said Buckeye, "then we shall have to tame him like a wild beast. . . ."

Kretyan's brother Kai spoke up. "It seems worth trying. Let some of us younger ones have charge of him; we'll see what we can do. We don't have to teach him the Inner Canons right away, after all. At least teaching him not to wet the bed comes first. . . . I want to know if he's human. Do you think he is, Master?"

Zove spread out his big hands. "Who knows? Rayna's blood-tests may tell us. I never heard that any Shing had yellow eyes, or any visible differences from Terran men. But if he is neither Shing nor human, what is he? No being from the Other Worlds that once were known has walked on Earth for twelve hundred years. Like you, Kai, I think I would risk his presence here among us out of pure curiosity. . . ."

So they let their guest live.

At first he was little trouble to the young people who looked after him. He regained strength slowly, sleeping much, sitting or lying quietly most of the time he was awake. Parth named him Falk, which in the dialect of the Eastern Forest meant "yellow," for his sallow skin and opal eyes.

One morning several days after his arrival, coming to an unpatterned stretch in the cloth she was weaving, she left her sunpowered loom to purr away by itself down in the garden and climbed up to the screened balcony where "Falk" was kept. He did not see her enter. He was sitting on his pallet gazing intently up at the haze-dimmed summer sky. The glare made his eyes water and he rubbed them vigorously with his hand, then seeing his hand stared at it, the back and the palm. He clenched and extended the fingers, frowning. Then he raised his face again to the white glare of the sun and slowly, tentative, reached his open hand up towards it.

"That's the sun, Falk," Parth said. "Sun. . . ."

"Sun," he repeated, gazing at it, centered on it, the void and vacancy of his being filled with the light of the sun and the sound of its name.

So his education began.

Parth came up from the cellars and passing through the Old Kitchen saw Falk hunched up in one of the window-bays, alone, watching the snow fall outside the grimy glass. It was a tennight now since he had struck Rossa and they had to lock him up till he calmed down. Ever since then he had been dour and would not speak. It was strange to see his man's face dulled and blunted by a child's sulky obstinate suffering. "Come on in by the fire, Falk," Parth said, but did not stop to wait for him. In the great hall by the fire she did wait a little, then gave him up and looked for something to raise her own low spirits. There was nothing to do; the snow fell, all the faces were too familiar, all the books told of things long ago and far away that were no longer true. All around the silent House and its fields lay the silent forest, endless, monotonous, indifferent; winter after winter, and she would never leave this House, for where was there to go, what was there to do? . . .

On one of the empty tables Ranya had left her *tëanb*, a nat, keyed instrument, said to be of Hainish origin. Parth picked out a tune in the melancholic Stepped Mode of the Eastern Forest, then retuned the instrument to its native scale and began anew. She had no skill with the *tëanb* and found the notes slowly, singing the words, spinning them out to keep the melody going as she sought the next note.

> *Beyond the sound of wind in trees*
> *beyond the storm-enshadowed seas,*
> *on stairs of sunlit stone the fair*
> *daughters of Airek stands . . .*

8

She lost the tune, then found it again:

> ... *stands,*
> *silent, with empty hands.*

A legend who knew how old, from a world incredibly remote, its words and tune had been part of man's heritage for centuries. Parth sang on very softly, alone in the great firelit room, snow and twilight darkening the windows.

There was a sound behind her and she turned to see Falk standing there. There were tears in his strange eyes. He said, "Parth—stop—"

"Falk, what's wrong?"

"It hurts me," he said, turning away his face that so clearly revealed the incoherent and defenseless mind.

"What a compliment to my singing," she teased him, but she was moved, and sang no more. Later that night she saw Falk stand by the table on which the tëanb lay. He raised his hand to it but dared not touch it, as if fearing to release the sweet relentless demon within it that had cried out under Parth's hands and changed her voice to music.

"My child learns faster than yours," Parth said to her cousin Garra, "but yours grows faster. Fortunately."

"Yours is quite big enough," Garra agreed, looking down across the kitchen-garden to the brookside where Falk stood with Garra's year-old baby on his shoulder. The early summer afternoon sang with the shrilling of crickets and gnats. Parth's hair clung in black locks to her cheeks as she tripped and reset and tripped the catches of her loom. Above her patterning shuttle rose the heads and necks of a row of dancing herons, silver thread on gray. At seventeen she was the best weaver among the women. In winter her hands were always stained with the chemicals of which her threads and yarns were made and the dyes that colored them, and all summer she wove at her sunpowered loom the delicate and various stuff of her imagination.

"Little spider," said her mother nearby, "a joke is a joke. But a man is a man."

"And you want me to go along with Metock to Kathol's house and trade my heron-tapestry for a husband. I know," said Parth.

"I never said it—did I?" inquired her mother, and went weeding on away between the lettuce-rows.

Falk came up the path, the baby on his shoulder squinting in the glare and smiling benignly. He put her down on the grass and said, as if to a grown person, "It's hotter up here, isn't it?" Then turning to Parth with the grave candor that was characteristic of him he asked, "Is there an end to the Forest, Parth?"

"So they say. The maps are all different. But that way lies the sea at last—and that way the prairie."

"Prairie?"

"Open lands, grasslands. Like the Clearing but going on for a thousand miles to the mountains."

"The mountains?" he asked, innocently relentless as any child.

"High hills, with snow on their tops all year. Like this." Pausing to reset her shuttle, Parth put her long, round, brown fingers together in the shape of a peak.

Falk's yellow eyes lit up suddenly, and his face became intense. "Below the white is blue, and below that the— the lines—the hills far away—"

10

Parth looked at him, saying nothing. A great part of all he knew had come straight from her, for she had always been the one who could teach him. The remaking of his life had been an effect and a part of the growth of her own. Their minds were very closely interwoven.

"I see it—have seen it. I remember it," the man stammered.

"A projection, Falk?"

"No. Not from a book. In my mind. I do remember it. Sometimes going to sleep I see it. I didn't know its name: the Mountain."

"Can you draw it?"

Kneeling beside her he sketched quickly in the dust the outline of an irregular cone, and beneath it two lines of foothills. Garra craned to see the sketch, asking, "And it's white with snow?"

"Yes. It's as if I see it through something—a big window, big and high up. . . . Is it from your mind, Parth?" he asked a little anxiously.

"No," the girl said. "None of us in the House have ever seen high mountains. I think there are none this side of the Inland River. It must be far from here, very far." She spoke like one on whom a chill had fallen.

Through the edge of dreams a sawtooth sound cut, a faint jagged droning, eerie. Falk roused and sat up beside Parth; both gazed with strained, sleepy eyes northward where the remote sound throbbed and faded and first light paled the sky above the darkness of the trees. "An aircar," Parth whispered. "I heard one once before, long ago. . . ." She shivered. Falk put his arm around her shoulders, gripped by the same unease, the sense of a

11

remote, uncomprehended, evil presence passing off there in the north through the edge of daylight.

The sound died away; in the vast silence of the Forest a few birds piped up for the sparse dawn-chorus of autumn. Light in the east brightened. Falk and Parth lay back down in the warmth and the infinite comfort of each other's arms; only half wakened, Falk slipped back into sleep. When she kissed him and slipped away to go about the day's work he murmured, "Don't go yet . . . little hawk, little one . . ." But she laughed and slipped away, and he drowsed on a while, unable as yet to come up out of the sweet lazy depths of pleasure and of peace.

The sun shone bright and level in his eyes. He turned over, then sat up yawning and stared into the deep, red-leaved branches of the oak that towered up beside the sleeping-porch. He became aware that in leaving Parth had turned on the sleepteacher beside his pillow; it was muttering softly away, reviewing Cetian number theory. That made him laugh, and the cold of the bright November morning woke him fully. He pulled on his shirt and breeches—heavy, soft, dark cloth of Parth's weaving, cut and fitted for him by Buckeye—and stood at the wooden rail of the porch looking across the Clearing to the brown and red and gold of the endless trees.

Fresh, still, sweet, the morning was as it had been when the first people on this land had waked in their frail, pointed houses and stepped outside to see the sun rise free of the dark forest. Mornings are all one, and autumn always autumn, but the years men count are many. There had been a first race on this land . . . and a second, the conquerors; both were lost, conquered and conquerors, millions of lives, all drawn together to a vague point on the horizon of past time. The stars had been gained, and lost again. Still the years went on, so many years that the Forest of archaic times, destroyed utterly during the era when men had made and kept their history, had grown up again. Even in the obscure vast history of a planet the time it takes to make a forest counts. It takes a while. And not every planet can do it; it is no common effect, that tangling of the sun's first cool light in the shadow and complexity of innumerable wind-stirred branches. . . .

Falk stood rejoicing in it, perhaps the more intensely because for him behind this morning there were so few other mornings, so short a stretch of remembered days between him and the dark. He listened to the remarks made by a chickadee in the oak, then stretched, scratched his head vigorously, and went off to join the work and company of the house.

Zove's House was a rambling, towering, intermitted chalet-castle-farmhouse of stone and timber; some parts of it had stood a century or so, some longer. There was a primitiveness to its aspect: dark staircases, stone hearths and cellars, bare floors of tile or wood. But nothing in it was unfinished; it was perfectly fireproof and weather-proof; and certain elements of its fabric and function were highly sophisticated devices or machines—the pleasant, yellowish fusion-lights, the libraries of music, words and images, various automatic tools or devices used in house-cleaning, cooking, washing, and farmwork, and some subtler and more specialized instruments kept in workrooms in the East Wing. All these things were part of the House, built into it or along with it, made in it or in another of the Forest Houses. The machinery was heavy and simple, easy to repair; only the knowledge behind its power-source was delicate and irreplaceable.

One type of technological device was notably lacking. The library evinced a skill with electronics that had become practically instinctive; the boys liked to build little tellies to signal one another with from room to room. But there was no television, telephone, radio, telegraph transmitting or receiving beyond the Clearing. There were no instruments of communication over distance. There were a couple of homemade air-cushion sliders in the East Wing, but again they featured mainly in the boys' games. They were hard to handle in the woods, on wilderness trails. When people went to visit and trade at another House they went afoot, perhaps on horseback if the way was very long.

The work of the House and farm was light, no hard burden to anyone. Comfort did not rise above warmth and cleanliness, and the food was sound but monotonous. Life in the House had the drab levelness of communal existence, a clean, serene frugality. Serenity and monotony rose from isolation. Forty-four people lived here together. Kathol's House, the nearest, was nearly thirty miles to the south. Around the Clearing mile after mile uncleared, unexplored, indifferent, the forest went on. The wild forest, and over it the sky. There was no shutting out the inhuman here, no narrowing man's life, as in the cities of earlier ages, to within man's scope. To keep anything at all of a complex civilization intact here among so few was a singular and very perilous achievement, though to most of them it seemed quite natural: it was the way one did; no other way was known. Falk saw it a little differently than did the children of the House, for he must always be aware that he had come out of that immense unhuman wilderness, as sinister and solitary as any wild beast that roamed it, and that all he had learned

14

in Zove's House was like a single candle burning in a great field of darkness.

At breakfast—bread, goat's-milk cheese and brown ale—Metock asked him to come with him to the deerblinds for the day. That pleased Falk. The Elder Brother was a very skillful hunter, and he was becoming one himself; it gave him and Metock, at last, a common ground. But the Master intervened: "Take Kai today, my son. I want to talk with Falk."

Each person of the household had his own room for a study or workroom and to sleep in in freezing weather; Zove's was small, high, and light, with windows west and north and east. Looking across the stubble and fallow of the autumnal fields to the forest the Master said, "Parth first saw you there, near that copper beech, I think. Five and a half years ago. A long time! Is it time we talked?"

"Perhaps it is, Master," Falk said, diffident.

"It's hard to tell, but I guessed you to be about twenty-five when you first came. What have you now of those twenty-five years?"

Falk held out his left hand a moment: "A ring," he said.

"And the memory of a mountain?"

"The memory of a memory." Falk shrugged. "And often, as I've told you, I find for a moment in my mind the sound of a voice, or the sense of a motion, a gesture, a distance. These don't fit into my memories of my life here with you. But they make no whole, they have no meaning."

Zove sat down in the windowseat and nodded for Falk to do the same. "You had no growing to do; your gross motor skills were unimpaired. But even given that basis, you have learned with amazing quickness. I've wondered if the Shing, in controlling human genetics in the old days and weeding out so many as colonists, were selecting us for docility and stupidity, and if you spring from some mutant race that somehow escaped control. Whatever you were, you were a highly intelligent man. . . . And now you are one again. And I should like to know what you yourself think about your mysterious past."

Falk was silent a minute. He was a short, spare, well-made man; his very lively and expressive face just now looked rather somber or apprehensive, reflecting his feelings as candidly as a child's face. At last, visibly summoning up his resolution, he said, "While I was studying with Ranya this past summer, she showed me how I differ from the human genetic norm. It's only a twist or two of a helix . . . a very small difference. Like the difference between *wei* and *o*." Zove looked up with a smile at the reference to the Canon which fascinated Falk, but the younger man was not smiling. "However, I am unmistakably not human. So I may be a freak; or a mutant, accidental or intentionally produced; or an alien. I suppose most likely I am an unsuccessful genetic experiment, discarded by the experimenters. . . . There's no telling. I'd prefer to think I'm an alien, from some other world. It would mean that at least I'm not the only creature of my kind in the universe."

"What makes you sure there are other populated worlds?"

Falk looked up, startled, going at once with a child's credulity but a man's logic to the conclusion: "Is there reason to think the other Worlds of the League were destroyed?"

"Is there reason to think they ever existed?"

"So you taught me yourself, and the books, the histories—"

"You believe them? You believe all we tell you?"

"What else can I believe?" He flushed red. "Why would you lie to me?"

"We might lie to you day and night about everything, for either of two good reasons. Because we are Shing. Or because we think you serve them."

There was a pause. "And I might serve them and never know it," Falk said, looking down.

"Possibly," said the Master. "You must consider that possibility, Falk. Among us, Metock has always believed you to be a programmed mind, as they call it. —But all the same, he's never lied to you. None of us has, knowingly. The River Poet said a thousand years ago, 'In truth manhood lies. . . .'" Zove rolled the words out oratorically, then laughed. "Double-tongued, like all poets. Well, we've told you what truths and facts we know, Falk. But perhaps not all the guesses and the legends, the stuff that comes before the facts. . . ."

"How could you teach me those?"

"We could not. You learned to see the world somewhere else—some other world, maybe. We could help you become a man again, but we could not give you a true childhood. That one has only once. . . ."

"I feel childish enough, among you," Falk said with a somber ruefulness.

"You're not childish. You are an inexperienced man. You are a cripple, because there *is* no child in you, Falk; you are cut off from your roots, from your source. Can you say that this is your home?"

"No," Falk answered, wincing. Then he said, "I have been very happy here."

17

The Master paused a little, but returned to his questioning. "Do you think our life here is a good one, that we follow a good way for men to go?"

"Yes."

"Tell me another thing. Who is our enemy?"

"The Shing."

"Why?"

"They broke the League of All Worlds, took choice and freedom from men, wrecked all man's works and records, stopped the evolution of the race. They are tyrants, and liars."

"But they don't keep us from leading our good life here."

"We're in hiding—we live apart, so that they'll let us be. If we tried to build any of the great machines, if we gathered in groups or towns or nations to do any great work together, then the Shing would infiltrate and ruin the work and disperse us. I tell you only what you told me and I believed, Master!"

"I know. I wondered if behind the fact you had perhaps sensed the . . . legend, the guess, the hope. . . ."

Falk did not answer.

"We hide from the Shing. Also we hide from what we were. Do you see that, Falk? We live well in the Houses —well enough. But we are ruled utterly by fear. There was a time we sailed in ships between the stars, and now we dare not go a hundred miles from home. We keep a little knowledge, and do nothing with it. But once we used that knowledge to weave the pattern of life like a tapestry across night and chaos. We enlarged the chances of life. We did man's work."

After another silence Zove went on, looking up into the bright November sky: "Consider the worlds, the various

18

men and beasts on them, the constellations of their skies, the cities they built, their songs and ways. All that is lost, lost to us, as utterly as your childhood is lost to you. What do we really know of the time of our greatness? A few names of worlds and heroes, a ragtag of facts we've tried to patch into a history. The Shing law forbids killing, but they killed knowledge, they burned books, and what may be worse, they falsified what was left. They slipped in the Lie, as always. We aren't sure of anything concerning the Age of the League; how many of the documents are forged? You must remember, you see, wherein the Shing are our Enemy. It's easy enough to live one's whole life without ever seeing one of them—knowingly; at most one hears an aircar passing by far away. Here in the Forest they let us be, and it may be the same now all over the Earth, though we don't know. They let us be so long as we stay here, in the cage of our ignorance and the wilderness, bowing when they pass by above our heads. But they don't trust us. How could they, even after twelve hundred years? There is no trust in them, because there is no truth in them. They honor no compact, break any promise, perjure, betray and lie inexhaustibly; and certain records from the time of the Fall of the League hint that they could mindlie. It was the Lie that defeated all the races of the League and left us subject to the Shing. Remember that, Falk. Never believe the truth of anything the Enemy has said."

"I will remember, Master, if I ever meet the Enemy."

"You will not, unless you go to them."

The apprehensiveness in Falk's face gave way to a listening, still look. What he had been waiting for had arrived. "You mean leave the House," he said.

"You have thought of it yourself," Zove said as quietly.

"Yes, I have. But there is no way for me to go. I want to live here. Parth and I—"

He hesitated, and Zove struck in, incisive and gentle. "I honor the love grown between you and Parth, your joy and your fidelity. But you came here on the way to somewhere else, Falk. You are welcome here; you have always been welcome. Your partnership with my daughter must be childless; even so, I have rejoiced in it. But I do believe that the mystery of your being and your coming here is a great one, not lightly to be put aside; that you walk a way that leads on; that you have work to do . . ."

"What work? Who can tell me?"

"What was kept from us and stolen from you, the Shing will have. That you can be sure of."

There was an aching, scathing bitterness in Zove's voice that Falk had never heard.

"Will those who speak no truth tell me the truth for the asking? And how will I recognize what I seek when I find it?"

Zove was silent a little while, and then said with his usual ease and control, "I cling to the notion, my son, that in you lies some hope for man. I do not like to give up that notion. But only you can seek your own truth; and if it seems to you that your way ends here, then that, perhaps, *is* the truth."

"If I go," Falk said abruptly, "will you let Parth go with me?"

"No, my son."

A child was singing down in the garden—Garra's four-year-old, turning inept somersaults on the path and singing shrill, sweet nonsense. High up, in the long wavering

V of the great migrations, skein after skein of wild geese went over southward.

"I was to go with Metock and Thurro to fetch home Thurro's bride," Falk said. "We planned to go soon, before the weather changes. If I go, I'll go on from Ransifel House."

"In winter?"

"There are Houses west of Ransifel, no doubt, where I can ask shelter if I need it."

He did not say and Zove did not ask why west was the direction he would go.

"There may be; I don't know. I don't know if they would give shelter to strangers as we do. If you go you will be alone, and must be alone. Outside this House there is no safe place for you on Earth."

He spoke, as always, absolutely truthfully . . . and paid the cost of truth in self-control and pain. Falk said with quick reassurance, "I know that, Master. It's not safety I'd regret—"

"I will tell you what I believe about you. I think you came from a lost world; I think you were not born on Earth. I think you came here, the first Alien to return in a thousand years or more, bringing us a message or a sign. The Shing stopped your mouth, and turned you loose in the forests so that none might say they had killed you. You came to us. If you go I will grieve and fear for you, knowing how alone you go. But I will hope for you, and for ourselves! If you had words to speak to men, you'll remember them, in the end. There must be a hope, a sign: we cannot go on like this forever."

"Perhaps my race was never a friend of mankind," Falk said, looking at Zove with his yellow eyes. "Who knows what I came here to do?"

"You'll find those who know. And then you'll do it. I don't fear it. If you serve the Enemy, so do we all: all's lost and nothing's to lose. If not, then you have what we men have lost: a destiny; and in following it you may bring hope to us all. . . ."

II

ZOVE HAD LIVED sixty years, Parth twenty; but she seemed, that cold afternoon in the Long Fields, old in a way no man could be old, ageless. She had no comfort from ideas of ultimate star-spanning triumph or the prevalence of truth. Her father's prophetic gift in her was only lack of illusion. She knew Falk was going. She said only, "You won't come back."

"I will come back, Parth."

She held him in her arms but she did not listen to his promise.

He tried to bespeak her, though he had little skill in telepathic communication. The only Listener in the house was blind Kretyan; none of them was adept at the non-verbal communication, mindspeech. The techniques of learning mindspeech had not been lost, but they were little practiced. The great virtue of that most intense and perfect form of communication had become its peril for men.

Mindspeech between two intelligences could be inco-herent or insane, and could of course involve error, misbelief; but it could not be misused. Between thought and spoken word is a gap where intention can enter, the symbol be twisted aside, and the lie come to be. Between thought and sent-thought is no gap; they are one act. There is no room for the lie.

In the late years of the League, the tales and fragmentary records Falk had studied seemed to show, the use of mind-speech had been widespread and the telepathic skills very highly developed. It was a skill Earth had come to late, learning its techniques from some other race; the Last Art, one book called it. There were hints of troubles and upheavals in the government of the League of All Worlds, rising perhaps from that prevalence of a form of communication that precluded lying. But all that was vague and half-legendary, like all man's history. Certainly since the coming of the Shing and the downfall of the League, the scattered community of man had mistrusted trust and used the spoken word. A free man can speak freely, but a slave or fugitive must be able to hide truth and lie. So Falk had learned in Zove's House, and so it was that he had had little practice in the attunement of minds. But he tried now to bespeak Parth so she would know he was not lying: "Believe me, Parth, I will come back to you!"

But she wouldn't hear. "No, I won't mindspeak," she said aloud.

"Then you're keeping your thoughts from me."

"Yes, I am. Why should I give you my grief? What's the good of truth? If you had lied to me yesterday, I'd still believe that you were only going to Ransifel and would be back home in a tennight. Then I'd still have ten days and nights. Now I have nothing left, not a day, not an hour. It's all taken, all over. What good is truth?"

24

"Parth, will you wait for me one year?"

"No."

"Only a year—"

"A year and a day, and you'll return riding a silver steed to carry me to your kingdom and make me its queen. No, I won't wait for you, Falk. Why must I wait for a man who will be lying dead in the forest, or shot by Wanderers out on the prairie, or brainless in the City of the Shing, or gone off a hundred years to another star? What should I wait for? You needn't think I'll take another man. I won't. I'll stay here in my father's house. I'll dye black thread and weave black cloth to wear, black to wear and black to die in. But I won't wait for anyone, or anything. Never."

"I had no right to ask you," he said with the humility of pain—and she cried, "O Falk, I don't reproach you!"

They were sitting together on the slight slope above the Long Field. Goats and sheep grazed over the mile of fenced pasture between them and the forest. Yearling colts pranced and tagged around the shaggy mares. A gray November wind blew.

Their hands lay together. Parth touched the gold ring on his left hand. "A ring is a thing given," she said. "Sometimes I've thought, have you? that you may have had a wife. Think, if she was waiting for you. . . ." She shivered.

"What of it?" he said. "What do I care about what may have been, what I was? Why should I go from here? All that I am now is yours, Parth, came from you, your gift—"

"It was freely given," the girl said in tears. "Take it and go. Go on. . . ." They held each other, and neither would break free.

The House lay far behind hoar black trunks and inter-
tangling leafless branches. The trees closed in behind the
trail.

The day was gray and cool, silent except for the drone
of wind through branches, a meaningless whisper without locality that never ceased. Metock led the way, setting a long easy pace. Falk followed and young Thurro
came last. They were all three dressed light and warm in
hooded shirt and breeches of an unwoven stuff called
wintercloth, over which no coat was needed even in
snow. Each carried a light backpack of gifts and trade-
goods, sleeping-bag, enough dried concentrated food to
see him through a month's blizzard. Buckeye, who had
never left the House of her birth, had a great fear of
perils and delays in the Forest and had supplied their
packs accordingly. Each wore a laser-beam gun; and
Falk carried some extras—another pound or two of food;
medicines, compass, a second gun, a change of clothing,
a coil of rope; a little book given him two years ago by
Zove—amounting in all to about fifteen pounds of stuff,
his earthly possessions. Easy and tireless Metock loped on
ahead, and ten yards or so behind he followed, and after
him came Thurro. They went lightly, with little sound,
and behind them the trees gathered motionless over the
faint, leaf-strewn trail.

They would come to Ransifel on the third day. At evening of the second day they were in country different
from that around Zove's House. The forest was more
open, the ground broken. Gray glades lay along hillsides
above brush-choked streams. They made camp in one of
these open places, on a south-facing slope, for the north
wind was blowing stronger with a hint of winter in it.
Thurro brought armloads of dry wood while the other

two cleared away the gray grass and piled up a rough hearth of stones. As they worked Metock said, "We crossed a divide this afternoon. The stream down there runs west. To the Inland River, finally."

Falk straightened up and looked westward, but the low hills rose up soon and the low sky closed down, leaving no distant view.

"Metock," he said, "I've been thinking there's no point in my going on to Ransifel. I may as well be on my way. There seemed to be a trail leading west along the big stream we crossed this afternoon. I'll go back and follow it."

Metock glanced up; he did not mindspeak, but his thought was plain enough: *Are you thinking of running back home?*

Falk did use mindspeech for his reply: "No, damn it, I'm not!"

"I'm sorry," the Elder Brother said aloud, in his grim, scrupulous way. He had not tried to hide the fact that he was glad to see Falk go. To Metock nothing mattered much but the safety of the House; any stranger was a threat, even the stranger he had known for five years, his hunting-companion and his sister's lover. But he went on, "They'll make you welcome at Ransifel. Why not start from there?"

"Why not from here?"

"Your choice." Metock worked a last rock into place, and Falk began to build up the fire. "If that was a trail we crossed, I don't know where it comes from or goes. Early tomorrow we'll cross a real path, the old Hirand Road. Hirand House was a long way west, a week on foot at least; nobody's gone there for sixty or seventy years. I don't know why. But the trail was still plain last time I came this way. The other might be an animal track, and lead you straying or leave you in a swamp."

"All right, I'll try the Hirand Road."

There was a pause, then Metock asked, "Why are you going west?"

"Because Es Toch is in the west."

The name seldom spoken sounded flat and strange out here under the sky. Thurro coming up with an armload of wood glanced around uneasily. Metock asked nothing more.

That night on the hillside by the campfire was Falk's last with those who were to him his brothers, his own people. Next morning they were on the trail again a little after sunrise, and long before noon they came to a wide, overgrown trace leading to the left off the path to Ransifel. There was a kind of gateway to it made by two great pines. It was dark and still under their boughs where they stopped.

"Come back to us, guest and brother," young Thurro said, troubled even in his bridegroom's self-absorption by the look of that dark, vague way Falk would be taking. Metock said only, "Give me your water-flask, will you," and in exchange gave Falk his own flask of chased silver. Then they parted, they going north and he west.

After he had walked a while Falk stopped and looked back. The others were out of sight; the Ransifel trail was already hidden behind the young trees and brush that overgrew the Hirand Road. The road looked as though it was used, if infrequently, but had not been kept up or cleared for many years. Around Falk nothing was visible but the forest, the wilderness. He stood alone under the shadows of the endless trees. The ground was soft with the fall of a thousand years; the great trees, pines and hemlocks, made the air dark and quiet. A fleck or two of sleet danced on the dying wind.

Falk eased the strap of his pack a bit and went on.

By nightfall it seemed to him that he had been gone from the House for a long, long time, that it was immeasurably far behind him, that he had always been alone.

His days were all the same. Gray winter light; a wind blowing; forest-clad hills and valleys, long slopes, brush-hidden streams, swampy lowlands. Though badly overgrown the Hirand Road was easy to follow, for it led in long straight shafts or long easy curves, avoiding the bogs and the heights. In the hills Falk realized it followed the course of some great ancient highway, for its way had been cut right through the hills, and two thousand years had not effaced it wholly. But the trees grew on it and beside it and all about it, pine and hemlock, vast holly-thickets on the slopes, endless stands of beech, oak, hickory, alder, ash, elm, all overtopped and crowned by the lordly chestnuts only now losing their last dark-yellow leaves, dropping their fat brown burrs along the path. At night he cooked the squirrel or rabbit or wild hen he had bagged from among the infinity of little game that scurried and flitted here in the kingdom of the trees; he gathered beechnuts and walnuts, roasted the chestnuts on his campfire coals. But the nights were bad. There were two evil dreams that followed him each day and always caught up with him by midnight. One was of being stealthily pursued in the darkness by a person he could never see. The other was worse. He dreamed that he had forgotten to bring something with him, something important, essential, without which he would be lost. From this dream he woke and knew that it was true: he was lost; it was himself he had forgotten. He would build up his fire then if it was not raining and would crouch beside it, too sleepy and dream-bemused to take up the book he carried, the Old Canon, and seek comfort in the words which declared that when all ways are lost the Way lies clear. A man all alone is a miserable thing. And he knew he was not even a man but at best a kind of half-being, trying to find his wholeness by setting out aimlessly to cross a continent under uninterested stars. The days were all the same, but they were a relief after the nights.

He was still keeping count of their number, and it was on the eleventh day from the crossroads, the thirteenth of his journey, that he came to the end of the Hirand Road. There had been a clearing, once. He found a way through great tracts of wild bramble and second-growth birch thickets to four crumbling black towers that stuck high up out of the brambles and vines and mummied thistles: the chimneys of a fallen House. Hirand was nothing now, a name. The road ended at the ruin.

He stayed around the fallen place a couple of hours, kept there simply by the bleak hint of human presence. He turned up a few fragments of rusted machinery, bits of broken pottery which outlive even men's bones, a scrap of rotten cloth which fell to dust in his hands. At last he pulled himself together and looked for a trail leading west out of the clearing. He came across a strange thing, a field a half-mile square covered perfectly level and smooth with some glassy substance, dark violet colored, unflawed. Earth was creeping over its edges and leaves and branches had scurfed it over, but it was unbroken, unscratched. It was as if the great level space had been flooded with melted amethyst. What had it been—a launching-field for some unimaginable vehicle, a mirror with which to signal other worlds, the basis of a force-field? Whatever it was, it had brought doom on Hirand. It had been a greater work than the Shing permitted men to undertake.

Falk went on past it and entered the forest, following no path now.

These were clean woods of stately, wide-aisled deciduous trees. He went on at a good pace the rest of that day, and the next morning. The country was growing hilly again, the ridges all running north-south across his way, and around ·noon, heading for what looked from one ridge like the low point of the next, he became embroiled in a marshy valley full of streams. He searched for fords, floundered in boggy watermeadows, all in a cold heavy rain. Finally as he found a way up out of the gloomy valley the weather began to break up, and as he climbed the ridge the sun came out ahead of him under the clouds and sent a wintry glory raying down among the naked branches, brightening them and the great trunks and the ground with wet gold. That cheered him; he went on sturdily, figuring to walk till day's end before he camped. Everything was bright now and utterly silent except for the drip of rain from twig-ends and the far-off wistful whistle of a chickadee. Then he heard, as in his dream, the steps that followed behind him to his left.

A fallen oak that had been an obstacle became in one startled moment a defense: he dropped down behind it and with drawn gun spoke aloud: "Come on out!"

For a long time nothing moved.

"Come out!" Falk said with the mindspeech, then closed to reception, for he was afraid to receive. He had a sense of strangeness; there was a faint, rank odor on the wind.

A wild boar walked out of the trees, crossed his tracks, and stopped to snuff the ground. A grotesque, magnificent pig, with powerful shoulders, razor back, trim, quick, filthy legs. Over snout and tusk and bristle, little bright eyes looked up at Falk.

"Aah, aah, aah, man, aah," the creature said, snuffling.

Falk's tense muscles jumped, and his hand tightened on the grip of his laser-pistol. He did not shoot. A wounded boar was hideously quick and dangerous. He crouched there absolutely still.

"Man, man," said the wild pig, the voice thick and flat from the scarred snout, "think to me. Think to me. Words are hard for me."

Falk's hand on the pistol shook now. Suddenly he spoke aloud: "Don't speak, then. I will not mindspeak. Go on, go your pig's way."

"Aah, aah, man, bespeak me!"

"Go or I will shoot." Falk stood up, his gun pointing steadily. The little bright hog-eyes watched the gun.

"It is wrong to take life," said the pig.

Falk had got his wits back and this time made no answer, sure that the beast understood no words. He moved the gun a little, recentered its aim, and said, "Go!" The boar dropped its head, hesitated. Then with incredible swiftness, as if released by a cord breaking, it turned and ran the way it had come.

Falk stood still a while, and when he turned and went on he kept his gun ready in his hand. His hand shook again, a little. There were old tales of beasts that spoke, but the people of Zove's House had thought them only tales. He felt a brief nausea and an equally brief wish to laugh out loud. "Parth," he whispered, for he had to talk to somebody, "I just had a lesson in ethics from a wild pig. . . . Oh, Parth, will I ever get out of the forest? Does it ever end?"

He worked his way on up the steepening, brushy slopes of the ridge. At the top the woods thinned out and through the trees he saw sunlight and the sky. A few paces more and he was out from under the branches, on the rim of a green slope that dropped down to a sweep of orchards and plow-lands and at last to a wide, clear river. On the far side of the river a herd of fifty or more cattle grazed in a long fenced meadow, above which hayfields and orchards rose steepening towards the tree-rimmed western ridge. A short way south of where Falk stood the river turned a little around a low knoll, over the shoulder of which, gilt by the low, late sun, rose the red chimneys of a house.

It looked like a piece of some other, golden age caught in that valley and overlooked by the passing centuries, preserved from the great wild disorder of the desolate forest. Haven, companionship, and above all, order: the work of man. A kind of weakness of relief filled Falk, at the sight of a wisp of smoke rising from those red chimneys. A hearthfire. . . . He ran down the long hillside and through the lowest orchard to a path that wandered along beside the riverbank among scrub alder and golden willows. No living thing was to be seen except the red-brown cattle grazing across the water. The silence of peace filled the wintry, sunlit valley. Slowing his pace, he walked between kitchen-gardens to the nearest door of the house. As he came around the knoll the place rose up before him, walls of ruddy brick and stone reflecting in the quickened water where the river curved. He stopped, a little daunted, thinking he had best hail the house aloud before he went any farther. A movement in an open window just above the deep doorway caught his eye. As he stood half hesitant, looking up, he felt a sudden deep, thin pain sear through his chest just below the breastbone: he staggered and then dropped, doubling up like a swatted spider.

The pain had been only for an instant. He did not lose consciousness, but he could not move or speak.

People were around him; he could see them, dimly, through waves of non-seeing, but could not hear any voices. It was as if he had gone deaf, and his body was entirely numb. He struggled to think through this deprivation of the senses. He was being carried somewhere and could not feel the hands that carried him; a horrible giddiness overwhelmed him, and when it passed he had lost all control of his thoughts, which raced and babbled and chattered. Voices began to gabble and drone inside his mind, though the world drifted and ebbed dim and silent about him. Who are you are you where do you come from Falk going where going are you I don't know are you a man west going I don't know where the way eyes a man not a man. . . . Waves and echoes and flights of words like sparrows, demands, replies, narrowing, overlapping, lapping, crying, dying away to a gray silence.

A surface of darkness lay before his eyes. An edge of light lay along it.

A table; the edge of a table. Lamp-lit, in a dark room. He began to see, to feel. He was in a chair, in a dark room, by a long table on which a lamp stood. He was tied into the chair: he could feel the cord cut into the muscles of his chest and arms as he moved a little. Movement: a man sprang into existence at his left, another at his right. They were sitting like him, drawn up to the table. They leaned forward and spoke to each other across him. Their voices sounded as if they came from behind high walls a great way off, and he could not understand the words.

He shivered with cold. With the sensation of cold he came more closely in touch with the world and began to regain control of his mind. His hearing was clearer, his tongue was loosed. He said something which was meant to be, "What did you do to me?"

There was no answer, but presently the man on his left stuck his face quite close to Falk's and said loudly, "Why did you come here?"

Falk heard the words; after a moment he understood them; after another moment he answered. "For refuge. The night."

"Refuge from what?"

"Forest. Alone."

He was more and more penetrated with cold. He managed to get his heavy, clumsy hands up a little, trying to button his shirt. Below the straps that bound him in the chair, just below his breastbone was a little painful spot.

"Keep your hands down," the man on his right said out of the shadows. "It's more than programming, Argerd. No hypnotic block could stand up to penton that way."

The one on his left, slab-faced and quick-eyed, a big man, answered in a weak sibilant voice: "You can't say that—what do we know about their tricks? Anyhow, how can you estimate his resistance—what is he? You, Falk, where is this place you came from, Zove's House?"

"East. I left . . ." The number would not come to mind. "Fourteen days ago, I think."

How did they know the name of his House, his name?

35

He was getting his wits back now, and did not wonder very long. He had hunted deer with Metock using hypodermic darts, which could make even a scratch-wound a kill. The dart that had felled him, or a later injection when he was helpless, had been some drug which must relax both the learned control and the primitive unconscious block of the telepathic centers of the brain, leaving him open to para-verbal questioning. They had ransacked his mind. At the idea, his feeling of coldness and sickness increased, complicated by helpless outrage. Why this violation? Why did they assume he would lie to them before they even spoke to him?

"Did you think I was a Shing?" he asked.

The face of the man on his right, lean, long-haired, bearded, sprang suddenly into the lamplight, the lips drawn back, and his open hand struck Falk across the mouth, jolting his head back and blinding him a moment with the shock. His ears rang; he tasted blood. There was a second blow and a third. The man kept hissing many times over. "You do not say that name, don't say it, you do not say it, you don't say it—"

Falk struggled helplessly to defend himself, to get free. The man on his left spoke sharply. Then there was silence for some while.

"I meant no harm coming here," Falk said at last, as steadily as he could through his anger, pain and fear.

"All right," said the one on the left, Argerd, "go on and tell your little story. What did you mean in coming here?"

"To ask for a night's shelter. And ask if there's any trail going west."

"Why are you going west?"

"Why do you ask? I told you in mindspeech, where there's no lying. You know my mind."

36

"You have a strange mind," Argerd said in his weak voice. "And strange eyes. Nobody comes here for a night's shelter or to ask the way or for anything else. Nobody comes here. When the servants of the Others come here, we kill them. We kill toolmen, and the speaking beasts, and Wanderers and pigs and vermin. We don't obey the law that says it's wrong to take life—do we, Drehnem?"

The bearded one grinned, showing brownish teeth.

"We are men," Argerd said. "Men, free men, killers. What are you, with your half-mind and your owl's eyes, and why shouldn't we kill you? Are you a man?"

In the brief span of his memory, Falk had not met directly with cruelty or hate. The few people he had known had been, if not fearless, not ruled by fear; they had been generous and familiar. Between these two men he knew he was defenseless as a child, and the knowledge both bewildered and enraged him.

He sought some defense or evasion and found none. All he could do was speak the truth. "I don't know what I am or where I came from. I'm going to try to find out."

"Going where?"

He looked from Argerd to the other one, Drehnem. He knew they knew the answer, and that Drehnam would strike again if he said it.

"Answer!" the bearded one muttered, half rising and leaning forward.

"To Es Toch," Falk said, and again Drehnem struck him across the face, and again he took the blow with the silent humiliation of a child punished by strangers.

"This is no good; he's not going to say anything different from what we got from him under penton. Let him up."

"Then what?" said Drehnem.

"He came for a night's shelter; he can have it. Get up!"

The strap that held him into the chair was loosened. He got shakily onto his feet. When he saw the low door and the black down-pitch of stairs they forced him towards, he tried to resist and break free, but his muscles would not yet obey him. Drehnem arm-twisted him down into a crouch and pushed him through the door way. The door slammed shut as he turned staggering to keep his footing on the stairs.

It was dark, black dark. The door was as if sealed shut, no handle on this side, no mote or hint of light coming under it, no sound. Falk sat down on the top step and put his head down on his arms.

Gradually the weakness of his body and the confusion in his mind wore off. He raised his head, straining to see. His night-vision was extraordinarily acute, a function, Ranna had long ago pointed out, of his large-pupiled, large-irised eyes. But only flecks and blurs of after-images tormented his eyes; he could see nothing, for there was no light. He stood up and step by step felt his slow way down the narrow, unseen descent.

Twenty-one steps, two, three—level. Dirt. Falk went slowly forward, one hand extended, listening.

Though the darkness was a kind of physical pressure, a constraint, deluding him constantly with the notion that if he only looked hard enough he would see, he had no fear of it in itself. Methodically, by pace and touch and hearing, he mapped out a part of the vast cellar he was in, the first room of a series which, to judge by echoes, seemed to go on indefinitely. He found his way directly back to the stairs, which because he had started from them were home base. He sat down, on the lowest step this time, and sat still. He was hungry and very thirsty. They had taken his pack, and left him nothing.

It's your own fault, Falk told himself bitterly, and a kind of dialogue began in his mind:

What did I do? Why did they attack me?

Zove told you: trust nobody. They trust nobody, and they're right.

Even someone who comes alone asking for help?

With your face—your eyes? When it's obvious even at a glance that you're not a normal human being?

All the same, they could have given me a drink of water, said the perhaps childish, still fearless part of his mind.

You're damned lucky they didn't kill you at sight, his intellect replied, and got no further answer.

All the people of Zove's House had of course got accustomed to Falk's looks, and guests were rare and circumspect, so that he had never been forced into particular awareness of his physical difference from the human norm. It had seemed so much less of a difference and barrier than the amnesia and ignorance that had isolated him so long. Now for the first time he realized that a stranger looking into his face would not see the face of a man.

The one called Drehnem had been afraid of him, and had struck him because he was afraid and repelled by the alien, the monstrous, the inexplicable.

It was only what Zove had tried to tell him when he had said with such grave and almost tender warning, "You must go alone, you can only go alone."

There was nothing for it, now, but sleep. He curled up as well as he could on the bottom step, for the dirt floor was damp, and closed his eyes on the darkness.

Some time later in timelessness he was awakened by the mice. They ran about making a faint tiny scrabble, a zigzag scratch of sound across the black, whispering in very small voices very close to the ground, "It is wrong to take life it is wrong to take life hello heeelllooo don't kill us don't kill."

"I will!" Falk roared and all the mice were still.

It was hard to go to sleep again; or perhaps what was hard was to be sure whether he was asleep or awake. He lay and wondered whether it was day or night; how long they would leave him here and if they meant to kill him, or use that drug again until his mind was destroyed, not merely violated; how long it took thirst to change from discomfort to torment; how one might go about catching mice in the dark without trap or bait; how long one could stay alive on a diet of raw mouse.

Several times, to get a vacation from his thoughts, he went exploring again. He found a great up-ended vat or tun and his heart leaped with hope, but it rang hollow: splintered boards near the bottom scratched his hands as he groped around it. He could find no other stairs or doors in his blind explorations of the endless unseen walls.

He lost his bearings finally and could not find the stairs again. He sat on the ground in the darkness and imagined rain falling, out in the forest of his lonely journeying, the gray light and the sound of rain. He spoke in his mind all he could remember of the Old Canon, beginning at the beginning:

*The way that can be gone
is not the eternal Way. . . .*

His mouth was so dry after a while that he tried to lick the damp dirt floor for its coolness; but to the tongue it was dry dust. The mice scuttled up quite close to him sometimes, whispering.

Far away down long corridors of darkness bolts clashed and metal clanged, a bright piercing clangor of light. Light—

Vague shapes and shadows, vaultings, arches, vats, beams, openings, bulked and loomed into dim reality about him. He struggled to his feet and made his way, unsteady but running, towards the light.

It came from a low doorway, through which, when he got close, he could see an upswell of ground, treetops, and the rosy sky of evening or morning, which dazzled his eyes like a midsummer noon. He stopped inside the door because of that dazzlement, and because a motionless figure stood just outside.

"Come out," said the weak, hoarse voice of the big man, Argerd.

"Wait. I can't see yet."

"Come out. And keep going. Don't even turn your head, or I'll burn it off your neck."

Falk came into the doorway, then hesitated again. His thoughts in the dark served some purpose now. If they did let him go, he had thought, it would mean that they were afraid to kill him.

"Move!"

He took the chance. "Not without my pack," he said, his voice faint in his dry throat.

"This is a laser."

41

"You might as well use it. I can't get across the continent without my own gun."

Now it was Argerd who hesitated. At last, his voice going up almost into a shriek, he yelled to someone: "Gretten! Gretten! Bring the stranger's stuff down here!"

A long pause. Falk stook in the darkness just inside the door, Argerd, motionless, just outside it. A boy came running down the grassy slope visible from the door, tossed Falk's pack down and disappeared.

"Pick it up," Argerd ordered; Falk came out into the light and obeyed. "Now get going."

"Wait," Falk muttered, kneeling and looking hastily through the disarrayed, unstrapped pack. "Where's my book?"

"Book?"

"The Old Canon. A handbook, not electronic—"

"You think we'd let you leave here with that?"

Falk stared. "Don't you people recognize the Canons of Man when you see them? What did you take it for?"

"You don't know and won't find out what we know, and if you don't get going I'll burn your hands off. Get up and go on, go straight on, get moving!" The shrieking note was in Argerd's voice again, and Falk realized he had nearly driven him too far. As he saw the look of hate and fear in Argerd's heavy, intelligent face the contagion of it caught him, and hastily he closed and shouldered his pack, walked past the big man and started up the grassy rise from the door of the cellars. The light was that of evening, a little past sunset. He walked towards it. A fine elastic strip of pure suspense seemed to connect the back of his head to the nose of the laserpistol Argerd held, stretching out, stretching out as he walked on. Across a weedy lawn, across a bridge of loose planks over the river, up a path between the pastures and then between orchards. He reached the top of the ridge. There he glanced back for one moment, seeing the hidden valley as he had first seen it, full of a golden evening light, sweet and peaceful, high chimneys over the sky-reflecting river. He hastened on into the gloom of the forest, where it was already night.

Thirsty and hungry, sore and downhearted, Falk saw his aimless journey through the Eastern Forest stretching on ahead of him with no vague hope, now, of a friendly hearth somewhere along the way to break the hard, wild monotony. He must not seek a road but avoid all roads, and hide from men and their dwellingplaces like any wild beast. Only one thing cheered him up a bit, besides a creek to drink from and some travel-ration from his pack, and that was the thought that though he had brought his trouble on himself, he had not knuckled under. He had bluffed the moral boar and the brutal man on their own ground, and got away with it. That did hearten him; for he knew himself so little that all his acts were also acts of self-discovery, like those of a boy, and knowing that he lacked so much he was glad to learn that at least he was not without courage.

After drinking and eating and drinking again he went on, in a broken moonlight that sufficed his eyes, till he had put a mile or so of broken country between himself and the house of Fear, as he thought of the place. Then, worn out, he lay down to sleep at the edge of a little glade, building no fire or shelter, lying gazing up at the moon-washed winter sky. Nothing broke the silence but now and again the soft query of a hunting owl. And this desolation seemed to him restful and blessed after the scurrying, voice-haunted, lightless prison-cellar of the house of Fear.

As he pushed on westward through the trees and the days, he kept no more count of one than of the other. Time went on; and he went on.

The book was not the only thing he had lost; they had kept Metock's silver water-flask, and a little box, also of silver, of disinfectant salve. They could only have kept the book because they wanted it badly, or because they took it for some kind of code or mystery. There was a period when the loss of it weighed unreasonably on him, for it seemed to him it had been his one true link with the people he had loved and trusted, and once he told himself, sitting by his fire, that next day he would turn back and find the house of Fear again and get his book. But he went on, next day. He was able to go west, with compass and sun for guides, but could never have refound a certain place in the vastness of these endless hills and valleys of the Forest. Not Argerd's hidden valley; not the Clearing where Parth might be weaving in the winter sunlight, either. It was all behind him, lost.

Maybe it was just as well that the book was gone. What would it have meant to him here, that shrewd and patient mysticism of a very ancient civilization, that quiet voice speaking from amidst forgotten wars and disasters? Mankind had outlived disaster; and he had outrun mankind. He was too far away, too much alone. He lived entirely now by hunting; that slowed his daily pace. Even when game is not gunshy and is very plentiful, hunting is not a business one can hurry. Then one must clean and cook the game, and sit and suck the bones beside the fire, full-bellied for a while and drowsy in the winter cold; and build up a shelter of boughs and bark against the rain; and sleep; and next day go on. A book had no place here, not even that old canon of Unaction. He would not have read it; he was ceasing, really, to think. He hunted and ate and walked and slept, silent in the forest silence, a gray shadow slipping westward through the cold wilderness.

The weather was more and more often bleak. Often lean feral cats, beautiful little creatures with their pied or striped fur and green eyes, waited within sight of his campfire for the leavings of his meat, and came forward with sly, shy fierceness to carry off the bones he tossed them: their rodent prey was scarce now, hibernating through the cold. No beasts since the house of Fear had spoken to or bespoken him. The animals in the lovely, icy, lowland woods he was now crossing had never been tampered with, had never seen or scented man, perhaps. And as it fell farther and farther behind him he saw its strangeness more clearly, that house hidden in its peaceful valley, its very foundations alive with mice that squeaked in human speech, its people revealing a great knowledge, the truth-drug, and a barbaric ignorance. The Enemy had been there.

That the Enemy had ever been here was doubtful. Nobody had ever been here. Nobody ever would be. Jays screamed in the gray branches. Frost-rimed brown leaves crackled underfoot, the leaves of hundreds of autumns. A tall stag looked at Falk across a little meadow, motionless, questioning his right to be there.

"I won't shoot you. Bagged two hens this morning," Falk said.

The stag stared at him with the lordly self-possession of the speechless, and walked slowly off. Nothing feared Falk, here. Nothing spoke to him. He thought that in the end he might forget speech again and become as he had been, dumb, wild, unhuman. He had gone too far away from men and had come where the dumb creatures ruled and men had never come.

At the meadow's edge he stumbled over a stone, and on hands and knees read weatherworn letters carved in the half-buried block: CK O.

Men had come here; had lived here. Under his feet, under the icy, hummocky terrain of leafless bush and naked tree, under the roots, there was a city. Only he had come to the city a millennium or two too late.

III

THE DAYS of which Falk kept no count had grown very
short, and had perhaps already passed Year's End, the
winter solstice. Though the weather was not so bad as it
might have been in the years when the city had stood
aboveground, this being a warmer meteorological cycle,
still it was mostly bleak and gray. Snow fell often, not so
thickly as to make the going hard, but enough to make
Falk know that if he had not had his wintercloth clothing
and sleeping-bag from Zove's House he would have suffered more than mere discomfort from the cold. The
north wind blew so unwearyingly bitter that he tended
always to be pushed a little southwards by it, picking the
way south of west when there was a choice, rather than
face into the wind.

In the dark wretched afternoon of one day of sleet and rain he came slogging down a south-trending stream-valley, struggling through thick brambly undergrowth over rocky, muddy ground. All at once the brush thinned out, and he was brought to a sudden halt. Before him lay a great river, dully shining, peppered with rain. Rainy mist half obscured the low farther bank. He was awed by the breadth, the majesty of this great silent westward drive of dark water under the low sky. At first he thought it must be the Inland River, one of the few landmarks of the inner continent known by rumor to the eastern Forest Houses; but that was said to run south marking the western edge of the kingdom of the trees. Surely it was a tributary of the Inland River, then. He followed it, for that reason, and because it kept him out of the high hills and provided both water and good hunting; moreover it was pleasant to have, sometimes, a sandy shore for a path, with the open sky overhead instead of the everlasting leafless darkness of branches. So following the river he went west by south through a rolling land of woods, all cold and still and colorless in the grip of winter.

One of these many mornings by the river he shot a wild hen, so common here in their squawking, low-flying flocks that they provided his staple meat. He had only winged the hen and it was not dead when he picked it up. It beat its wings and cried in its piercing bird-voice, "Take—life—take—life—take—" Then he wrung its neck.

The words rang in his mind and would not be silenced. Last time a beast had spoken to him he had been on the threshold of the house of Fear. Somewhere in these lonesome gray hills there were, or had been, men: a group in hiding like Argerd's household, or savage Wanderers who would kill him when they saw his alien eyes, or toolmen who would take him to their Lords as a prisoner or slave. Though at the end of it all he might have to face those Lords, he would find his own way to them, in his own time, and alone. Trust no one, avoid men! He knew his lesson now. Very warily he went that day, alert, so quiet that often the waterbirds that thronged the shores of the river rose up startled almost under his feet.

He crossed no path and saw no sign at all that any human beings dwelt or ever came near the river. But towards the end of the short afternoon a flock of the bronze-green wild fowl rose up ahead of him and flew out over the water all clucking and calling together in a gabble of human words.

A little farther on he stopped, thinking he had scented woodsmoke on the wind.

The wind was blowing upriver to him, from the northwest. He went with double caution. Then as the night rose up among the tree-trunks and blurred the dark reaches of the river, far ahead of him along the brushy, willow-tangled shore a light glimmered, and vanished, and shone again.

It was not fear or even caution that stopped him now, standing in his tracks to stare at that distant glimmer. Aside from his own solitary campfire this was the first light he had seen lit in the wilderness since he had left the Clearing. It moved him very strangely, shining far off there across the dusk.

Patient in his fascination as any forest animal, he waited till full night had come and then made his way slowly and noiselessly along the riverbank, keeping in the shelter of the willows, until he was close enough to see the square of a window yellow with firelight and the peak of the roof above it, snow-rimmed, pine-overhung. Huge over black forest and river Orion stood. The winter night was very cold and silent. Now and then a fleck of dry snow dislodged from a branch drifted down towards the black water and caught the sparkle of the firelight as it fell.

Falk stood gazing at the light in the cabin. He moved a little closer, then stood motionless for a long time.

The door of the cabin creaked open, laying down a fan of gold on the dark ground, stirring up powdery snow in puffs and spangles. "Come on into the light," said a man standing, vulnerable, in the golden oblong of the doorway.

Falk in the darkness of the thickets put his hand on his laser, and made no other movement.

"I mindheard you. I'm a Listener. Come on. Nothing to fear here. Do you speak this tongue?"

Silence.

"I hope you do, because I'm not going to use mindspeech. There's nobody here but me, and you," said the quiet voice. "I hear without trying, as you hear with your ears, and I still hear you out there in the dark. Come and knock if you want to get under a roof for a while."

The door closed.

Falk stood still for some while. Then he crossed the few dark yards to the door of the little cabin, and knocked.

"Come in!"

He opened the door and entered into warmth and light.

An old man, gray hair braided long down his back, knelt at the hearth building up the fire. He did not turn to look at the stranger, but laid his firewood methodically. After a while he said aloud in a slow chant,

50

> *"I alone am confused*
> *confused*
> *desolate*
> *Oh, like the sea*
> *adrift*
> *Oh, with no harbor*
> *to anchor in. . . ."*

The gray head turned at last. The old man was smiling; his narrow, bright eyes looked sidelong at Falk.

In a voice that was hoarse and hesitant because he had not spoken any words for a long time, Falk replied with the next verse of the Old Canon:

> *"Everyone is useful*
> *only I alone*
> *am inept*
> *outlandish.*
> *I alone differ from others*
> *but I seek*
> *the milk of the Mother*
> *the Way. . . ."*

"Ha ha ha!" said the old man. "Do you, Yellow-eyes? Come on, sit down, here by the hearth. Outlandish, yes yes, yes indeed. You are outlandish. How far out the land?—who knows? How long since you washed in hot water? Who knows? Where's the damned kettle? Cold tonight in the wide world, isn't it, cold as a traitor's kiss. Here we are; fill that from the pail there by the door, will you, then I'll put it on the fire, so. I'm a Thurro-dowist, you know what that is I see, so you won't get much comfort here. But a hot bath's hot, whether the kettle's

51

boiled with hydrogen fusion or pine-knots, eh? Yes, you really are outlandish, lad, and your clothes could use a bath too, weatherproof though they may be. What's that? —rabbits? Good. We'll stew 'em tomorrow with a vegetable or two. Vegetables are one thing you can't hunt down with a lasergun. And you can't store cabbages in a backpack. I live alone here, my lad, alone and all alonio. Because I am a great, a very great, the greatest Listener, I live alone, and talk too much. I wasn't born here, like a mushroom in the woods; but with other men I never could shut out the minds, all the buzz and grief and babble and worry and all the different ways they went, as if I had to find my way through forty different forests all at once. So I came to live alone in the real forest with only the beasts around me, whose minds are brief and still. No death lies in their thoughts. And no lies lie in their thoughts. Sit down; you've been a long time coming here and your legs are tired."

Falk sat down on the wooden hearth-bench. "I thank you for your hospitality," he said, and was about to name himself when the old man spoke: "Never mind. I can give you plenty of good names, good enough for this part of the world. Yellow Eyes, Outlander, Guest, anything will do. Remember I'm a Listener, not a paraverbalist. I get no words or names. I don't want them. That there was a lonely soul out there in the dark, I knew, and I know how my lighted window shone into your eyes. Isn't that enough, more than enough? I don't need names. And my name is All-Alonio. Right? Now pull up to the fire, get warm."

"I'm getting warm," Falk said.

The old man's gray braid flipped across his shoulders as he moved about, quick and frail, his soft voice running on; he never asked a real question, never paused for an answer. He was fearless and it was impossible to fear him.

Now all the days and nights of journeying through the forest drew together and were behind Falk. He was not camping: he had come to a place. He need not think at all about the weather, the dark, the stars and beasts and trees. He could sit stretching out his legs to a bright hearth, could eat in company with another, could bathe in front of the fire in a wooden tub of hot water. He did not know which was the greater pleasure, the warmth of that water washing dirt and weariness away, or the warmth that washed his spirit here, the absurd elusive vivid talk of the old man, the miraculous complexity of human conversation after the long silence of the wilderness.

He took as true what the old man told him, that he was able to sense Falk's emotions and perceptions, that he was a mindhearer, an empath. Empathy was to telepathy somewhat as touch to sight, a vaguer, more primitive, and more intimate sense. It was not subject to fine learned control to the degree that telepathic communication was; conversely, involuntary empathy was not uncommon even among the untrained. Blind Kretyan had trained herself to mindhear, having the gift by nature. But it was no such gift as this. It did not take Falk long to make sure that the old man was in fact constantly aware to some degree of what his visitor was feeling and sensing. For some reason this did not bother Falk, whereas the knowledge that Argerd's drug had opened his mind to telepathic search had enraged him. It was the difference in intent; and more.

"This morning I killed a hen," he said, when for a little

the old man was silent, warming a rough towel for him by the leaping fire. "It spoke, in this speech. Some words of . . . of the Law. Does that mean anyone is near here, who teaches language to the beasts and fowls?" He was not so relaxed, even getting out of the hot bath, as to say the Enemy's name—not after his lesson in the house of Fear.

By way of answer the old man merely asked a question for the first time: "Did you eat the hen?"

"No," said Falk, toweling himself dry in the firelight that reddened his skin to the color of new bronze. "Not after it talked. I shot the rabbits instead."

"Killed it and didn't eat it? Shameful, shameful." The old man cackled, then crowed like a wild cock. "Have you no reverence for life? You must understand the Law. It says you mustn't kill unless you must kill. And hardly even then. Remember that in Es Toch. Are you dry? Clothe your nakedness, Adam of the Yaweh Canon. Here, wrap this around you, it's no fine artifice like your own clothes, it's only deerhide tanned in piss, but at least it's clean."

"How do you know I'm going to Es Toch?" Falk asked, wrapping the soft leather robe about him like a toga.

"Because you're not human," said the old man. "And remember, I am the Listener. I know the compass of your mind, outlandish as it is, whether I will or no. North and south are dim; far back in the east is a lost brightness; to the west there lies darkness, a heavy darkness. I know that darkness. Listen. Listen to me, because I don't want to listen to you, dear guest and blunderer. If I wanted to listen to men talk I wouldn't live here among the wild pigs like a wild pig. I have this to say before I go to sleep. Now listen: There are not very many of the

54

Shing. That's a great piece of news and wisdom and advice. Remember it, when you walk in the awful darkness of the bright lights of Es Toch. Odd scraps of information may always come in handy. Now forget the east and west, and go to sleep. You take the bed. Though as a Thurro-dowist I am opposed to ostentatious luxury, I applaud the simpler pleasures of existence, such as a bed to sleep on. At least, every now and then. And even the company of a fellow man, once a year or so. Though I can't say I miss them as you do. Alone's not lonely. . . ." And as he made himself a sort of pallet on the floor he quoted in an affectionate singsong from the Younger Canon of his creed: " 'I am no more lonely than the mill brook, or a weathercock, or the north star, or the south wind, or an April shower, or a January thaw, or the first spider in a new house. . . . I am no more lonely than the loon on the pond that laughs so loud, or than Walden Pond itself. . . .' "

Then he said, "Good night!" and said no more. Falk slept that night the first sound, long sleep he had had since his journey had begun.

He stayed two more days and nights in the riverside cabin, for his host made him very welcome and he found it hard to leave the little haven of warmth and company. The old man seldom listened and never answered questions, but in and out of his ever-running talk certain facts and hints glanced and vanished. He knew the way west from here and what lay along it—for how far, Falk could not make sure. Clear to Es Toch, it seemed; perhaps even beyond? What lay beyond Es Toch? Falk himself had no idea, except that one would come eventually to the Western Sea, and on beyond that to the Great Continent, and eventually on around again to the Eastern Sea and the

Forest. That the world was round, men knew, but there were no maps left. Falk had a notion that the old man might have been able to draw one; but where he got such a notion he scarcely knew, for his host never spoke directly of anything he himself had done or seen beyond this little river-bank clearing.

"Look out for the hens, downriver," said the old man, apropos of nothing, as they breakfasted in the early morning before Falk set off again. "Some of them can talk. Others can listen. Like us, eh? I talk and you listen. Because, of course, I am the Listener and you are the Messenger. Logic be damned. Remember about the hens, and mistrust those that sing. Roosters are less to be mistrusted; they're too busy crowing. Go alone. It won't hurt you. Give my regards to any Princes or Wanderers you may meet, particularly Henstrella. By the way, it occurred to me in between your dreams and my own last night that you've walked quite enough for exercise and might like to take my slider. I'd forgotten I had it. I'm not going to use it, since I'm not going anywhere, except to die. I hope someone comes by to bury me, or at least drag me outside for the rats and ants, once I'm dead. I don't like the prospect of rotting around in here after all the years I've kept the place tidy. You can't use a slider in the forest, of course, now there are no trails left worth the name, but if you want to follow the river it'll take you along nicely. And across the Inland River too, which isn't easy to cross in the thaws, unless you're a catfish. It's in the lean-to if you want it. I don't."

The people of Kathol's House, the settlement nearest Zove's, were Thurro-dowists; Falk knew that one of their principles was to get along, as long as they could do so sanely and unfanatically, without mechanical devices and

artifices. That this old man, living much more primitively
than they, raising poultry and vegetables because he did
not even own a gun to hunt with, should possess a bit of
fancy technology like a slider, was queer enough to make
Falk for the first time look up at him with a shadow of
doubt.

The Listener sucked his teeth and cackled. "You never
had any reason to trust me, outlandish laddie," he said.
"Nor I you. After all, things can be hidden from even the
greatest Listener. Things can be hidden from a man's
own mind, can't they, so that he can't lay the hands of
thought upon them. Take the slider. My traveling days
are done. It carries only one, but you'll be going alone.
And I think you've got a longer journey to make than you
can ever go by foot. Or by slider, for that matter."

Falk asked no question, but the old man answered
it:

"Maybe you have to go back home," he said.

Parting from him in the icy, misty dawn under the ice-
furred pines, Falk in regret and gratitude offered his
hand as to the Master of a House; so he had been taught
to do; but as he did so he said, *"Tiokioi . . ."*

"What name do you call me, Messenger?"

"It means . . . it means *father*, I think. . . ." The word
had come on his lips unbidden, incongruous. He was not
sure he knew its meaning, and had no idea what language it was in.

"Goodbye, poor trusting fool! You will speak the truth
and the truth will set you free. Or not, as the case may
be. Go all alonio, dear fool; it's much the best way to go.
I will miss your dreams. Goodbye, goodbye. Fish and
visitors stink after three days. Goodbye!"

Falk knelt on the slider, an elegant little machine, black

paristolis inlaid with a three-dimensional arabesque of
platinum wire. The ornamentation all but concealed the
controls, but he had played with a slider at Zove's House,
and after studying the control-arcs a minute he touched
the left arc, moved his finger along it till the slider had
silently risen about two feet, and then with the right arc
sent the little craft slipping over the yard and the river-
bank till it hovered above the scummy ice of the back-
water below the cabin. He looked back then to call goodbye, but the old man had already gone into the cabin and
shut the door. And as Falk steered his noiseless craft
down the broad dark avenue of the river, the enormous
silence closed in around him again.

Icy mist gathered on the wide curves of water ahead of
him and behind him, and hung among the gray trees on
either bank. Ground and trees and sky were all gray with
ice and fog. Only the water sliding along a little slower
than he slid airborne above it was dark. When on the
following day snow began to fall the flakes were dark
against the sky, white against the water before they vanished, endlessly falling and vanishing in the endless current.

This mode of travel was twice the speed of walking,
and safer and easier—too easy indeed, monotonous,
hypnotic. Falk was glad to come ashore when he had to
hunt or to make camp. Waterbirds all but flew into his
hands, and animals coming down to the shore to drink
glanced at him as if he on the slider were a crane or
heron skimming past, and offered their defenseless flanks
and chests to his hunting gun. Then all he could do was
skin, hack up, cook, eat, and build himself a little shelter
for the night against snow or rain with boughs or bark

and the up-ended slider as a roof; he slept, at dawn ate cold meat left from last night, drank from the river, and went on. And on.

He played games with the slider to beguile the eventless hours: taking her up above fifteen feet where wind and air-layers made the aircushion unreliable and might tilt the slider right over unless he compensated instantly with the controls and his own weight; or forcing her down into the water in a wild commotion of foam and spray so she slapped and skipped and skittered all over the river, bucking like a colt. A couple of falls did not deter Falk from his amusements. The slider was set to hover at one foot if uncontrolled, and all he had to do was clamber back on, get to shore and make a fire if he had got chilled, or if not, simply go on. His clothes were weatherproof, and in any case the river could get him little wetter than the rain. The wintercloth kept him fairly warm; he was never really warm. His little campfires were strictly cookingfires. There was not enough dry wood in the whole Eastern Forest, probably, for a real fire, after the long days of rain, wet snow, mist, and rain again.

He became adept at slapping the slider downriver in a series of long, loud fish-leaps, diagonal bounces ending in a whack and a jet of spray. The noisiness of the process pleased him sometimes as a break in the smooth silent monotony of sliding along above the water between the trees and hills. He came whacking around a bend, banking his curves with delicate flicks of the control-arcs, then braked to a sudden soundless halt in mid-air. Far ahead down the steely-shining reach of the river a boat was coming towards him.

Each craft was in full view of the other; there was no

slipping past in secret behind screening trees. Falk lay flat on the slider, gun in hand, and steered down the right bank of the river, up at ten feet so he had height advantage on the people in the boat.

They were coming along easily with one little triangular sail set. As they drew nearer, though the wind was blowing downriver, he could faintly hear the sound of their singing.

They came still nearer, paying no heed to him, still singing.

As far back as his brief memory went, music had always both drawn him and frightened him, filling him with a kind of anguished delight, a pleasure too near torment. At the sound of a human voice singing he felt most intensely that he was not human, that his game of pitch and time and tone was alien to him. But by that strangeness it drew him, and now unconsciously he slowed the slider to listen. Four or five voices sang, chiming and parting and interweaving in a more artful harmony than any he had heard. He did not understand the words. All the forest, the miles of gray water and gray sky, seemed to him to listen in intense, uncomprehending silence.

The song died away, chiming and fading into a little gust of laughter and talk. The slider and the boat were nearly abreast now, separated by a hundred yards or more. A tall, very slender man erect in the stern hailed Falk, a clear voice ringing easily across the water. Again he caught none of the words. In the steely winter light the man's hair and the hair of the four or five others in the boat shone fulvent gold, all the same, as if they were all of one close kin, or one kind. He could not see the faces clearly, only the red-gold hair, the slender figures bending forward to laugh and beckon. He could not make sure how many there were. For a second one face was distinct, a woman's face, watching him across the moving water and the wind. He had slowed the slider to a hover, and the boat too seemed to rest motionless on the river.

"Follow us," the man called again, and this time, recognizing the language, Falk understood. It was the old League tongue, Galaktika. Like all Foresters, Falk had learned it from tapes and books, for the documents surviving from the Great Age were recorded in it, and it served as a common speech among men of different tongues. The Forest dialect was descended from Galaktika, but had grown far from it over a thousand years, and by now differed even from House to House. Travelers once had come to Zove's House from the coast of the Eastern Sea, speaking a dialect so divergent that they had found it easier to speak Galaktika with their hosts, and only then had Falk heard it used as a living tongue; otherwise it had only been the voice of a soundbook, or the murmur of the sleep teacher in his ear in the dark of a winter morning. Dreamlike and archaic it sounded now in the clear voice of the steersman. "Follow us, we go to the city!"

"To what city?"

"Our own," the man called, and laughed.

"The city that welcomes the traveler," another called; and another, in the tenor that had rung so sweetly in their singing, spoke more softly: "Those that mean no harm find no harm among us." And a woman called as if she smiled as she spoke, "Come out of the wilderness, traveler, and hear our music for a night."

The name they called him meant traveler, or messenger.

"Who are you?" he asked.

Wind blew and the broad river ran. The boat and the airboat hovered motionless amid the flow of air and water, together and apart as if in an enchantment.

"We are men."

With that reply the charm vanished, blown away like a sweet sound or fragrance in the wind from the east. Falk felt again a maimed bird struggle in his hands crying out human words in its piercing unhuman voice: now as then a chill went through him, and without hesitation, without decision, he touched the silver arc and sent the slider forward at full speed.

No sound came to him from the boat, though now the wind blew from them to him, and after a few moments, when hesitation had had time to catch up with him, he slowed his craft and looked back. The boat was gone. There was nothing on the broad dark surface of the water, clear back to the distant bend.

After that Falk played no more loud games, but went on as swiftly and silent as he might; he lit no fire at all that night, and his sleep was uneasy. Yet something of the charm remained. The sweet voices had spoken of a city, *Elonaae* in the ancient tongue, and drifting down-river alone in mid-air and mid-wilderness Falk whispered the word aloud. Elonaae, the Place of Man: myriads of men gathered together, not one house but thousands of houses, great dwelling-places, towers, walls, windows, streets and the open places where streets met, the trading-houses told of in books where all the ingenuities of men's hands were made and sold, the palaces of government where the mighty met to speak together of the great works they did, the fields from which ships shot out across the years to alien suns: had Earth ever borne so wonderful a thing as the Places of Man?

They were all gone now. There remained only Es Toch, the Place of the Lie. There was no city in the Eastern Forest. No towers of stone and steel and crystal crowded with souls rose up from among the swamps and alder-groves, the rabbit-warrens and deer-trails, the lost roads, the broken, buried stones.

Yet the vision of a city remained with Falk almost like the dim memory of something he had once known. By that he judged the strength of the lure, the illusion which he had blundered safely through, and he wondered if there would be more such tricks and lures as he went on always westward, towards their source.

The days and the river went on, flowing with him, until on one still gray afternoon the world opened slowly out and out into an awesome breadth, an immense plain of muddy waters under an immense sky: the confluence of the Forest River with the Inland River. It was no wonder they had heard of the Inland River even in the deep ignorance of their isolation hundreds of miles back east in the Houses: it was so huge even the Shing could not hide it. A vast and shining desolation of yellow-gray waters spread from the last crowns and islets of the flooded Forest on and on west to a far shore of hills. Falk soared like one of the river's low-flying blue herons over the meetingplace of the waters. He landed on the western bank and was, for the first time in his memory, out of the Forest.

To north, west, and south lay rolling land, clumped

with many trees, full of brush and thickets in the low-lands, but an open country, wide open. Falk with easy self-delusion looked west, straining his eyes to see the mountains. This open land, the Prairie, was believed to be very wide, a thousand miles perhaps; but no one in Zove's House really knew.

He saw no mountains, but that night he saw the rim of the world where it cut across the stars. He had never seen a horizon. His memory was all encircled with a boundary of leaves, of branches. But out here nothing was between him and the stars, which burned from the Earth's edge upwards in a huge bowl, a dome built of black patterned with fire. And beneath his feet the circle was completed; hour by hour the tilting horizon revealed the fiery patterns that lay eastward and beneath the Earth. He spent half the long winter night awake, and was awake again when that tilting eastern edge of the world cut across the sun and daylight struck from outer space across the plains.

That day he went on due west by the compass, and the next day, and the next. No longer led by the meanderings of the river, he went straight and fast. Running the slider was no such dull game as it had been over the water; here above uneven ground it bucked and tipped at each drop and rise unless he was very alert every moment at the controls. He liked the vast openness of sky and prairie, and found loneliness a pleasure with so immense a domain to be alone in. The weather was mild, a calm sunlit spell of late winter. Thinking back to the Forest he felt as if he had come out of stifling, secret darkness into light and air, as if the prairies were one enormous Clearing. Wild red cattle in herds of tens of thousands darkened the far plains like cloud-shadows. The ground was everywhere dark, but in places misted faintly with green where the first tiny double-leaved shoots of the hardiest grasses were opening; and above and below the ground was a constant scurrying and burrowing of little beasts, rabbits, badgers, coneys, mice, feral cats, moles, stripe-eyed arcturies, antelope, yellow yappers, the pests and pets of fallen civilizations. The huge sky whirred with wings. At dusk along the rivers flocks of white cranes settled, the water between the reeds and leafless cotton-woods mirroring their long legs and long uplifted wings.

Why did men no longer journey forth to see their world? Falk wondered, sitting by his campfire that burned like a tiny opal in the vast blue vault of the prairie twilight. Why did such men as Zove and Metock hide in the woods, never once in their lives coming out to see the wide splendor of the Earth? He now knew some-thing that they, who had taught him everything, did not know: that a man could see his planet turn among the stars. . . .

Next day under a lowering sky and through a cold wind from the north he went on, guiding the slider with a skill soon become habit. A herd of wild cattle covered half the plains south of his course, every one of the thou-sands and thousands of them standing facing the wind, white faces lowered in front of shaggy red shoulders. Between him and the first ranks of the herd for a mile the long gray grass bowed under the wind, and a gray bird flew towards him, gliding with no motion of its wings. He watched it, wondering at its straight gliding flight—not quite straight, for it turned without a wingbeat to inter-cept his course. It was coming very fast, straight at him. Abruptly he was alarmed, and waved his arm to frighten the creature away, then threw himself down flat and veered the slider, too late. The instant before it struck he saw the blind featureless head, the glitter of steel. Then the impact, a shriek of exploding metal, a sickening backward fall. And no end to the falling.

IV

"KESSNOKATY's old woman says it's going to snow," his friend's voice murmured near him. "We should be ready, if there comes a chance for us to run away."

Falk did not reply but sat listening with sharpened hearing to the noises of the camp: voices in a foreign tongue, distance-softened; the dry sound of somebody nearby scraping a hide; the thin bawl of a baby; the snapping of the tentfire.

"Horressins!" someone outside summoned him, and he got up promptly, then stood still. In a moment his friend's hand was on his arm and she guided him to where they wanted him, the communal fire in the center of the circle of tents, where they were celebrating a successful hunt by roasting a whole bull. A shank of beef was shoved into his hands. He sat down on the ground and began to eat. Juices and melted fat ran down his jaws but he did not wipe them off. To do so was beneath the dignity of a Hunter of the Mzurra Society of the Basnasska Nation. Though a stranger, a captive, and blind, he was a Hunter, and was learning to comport himself as such.

The more defensive a society, the more conformist. The people he was among walked a very narrow, a tortuous and cramped Way, across the broad free plains. So long as he was among them he must follow all the twistings of their ways exactly. The diet of the Basnasska consisted of fresh half-raw beef, raw onions, and blood. Wild herdsmen of the wild cattle, like wolves they culled the lame, the lazy and unfit from the vast herds, a lifelong feast of meat, a life with no rest. They hunted with hand-lasers and warded strangers from their territory with bombirds like the one that had destroyed Falk's slider, tiny impact-missiles programmed to home in on anything that contained a fusion element. They did not make or repair these weapons themselves, and handled them only after purifications and incantations; where they obtained them Falk had not found out, though there was occasional mention of a yearly pilgrimage, which might be connected with the weapons. They had no agriculture and no domestic animals; they were illiterate and did not know, except perhaps through certain myths and hero-legends, any of the history of humankind. They informed Falk that he had not come out of the Forest, because the Forest was inhabited only by giant white snakes. They practiced a monotheistic religion whose rituals involved mutilation, castration and human sacrifice.

It was one of the outgrowth-superstitions of their complex creed that had induced them to take Falk alive and make him a member of the tribe. Normally, since he carried a laser and thus was above slave-status, they would have cut out his stomach and liver to examine for auguries, and then let the women hack him up as they pleased. However, a week or two before his capture an old man of the Mzurra Society had died. There being no as-yet-unnamed infant in the tribe to receive his name, it was given to the captive, who, blinded, disfigured, and only conscious at intervals, still was better than nobody; for so long as Old Horressins kept his name his ghost, evil like all ghosts, would return to trouble the ease of the living. So the name was taken from the ghost and given to Falk, along with the full initiations of a Hunter, a ceremony which included whippings, emetics, dances, the recital of dreams, tattooing, antiphonal free-association, feasting, sexual abuse of one woman by all the males in turn, and finally nightlong incantations to The God to preserve the new Horressins from harm. After this they left him on a horsehide rug in a cowhide tent, delirious and unattended, to die or recover, while the ghost of Old Horressins, nameless and powerless, went whining away on the wind across the plains.

The woman, who, when he had first recovered consciousness, had been busy bandaging his eyes and looking after his wounds, also came whenever she could to care for him. He had only seen her when for brief moments in the semi-privacy of his tent he could lift the bandage which her quick wits had provided him when he was first brought in. Had the Basnasska seen those eyes of his open, they would have cut out his tongue so he could not name his own name, and then burned him alive. She had told him this, and other matters he needed to know about the Nation of the Basnasska; but not much about herself. Apparently she had not been with the tribe very much longer than himself; he gathered that she had been lost on the prairie, and had joined the tribe rather than starve to death. They were willing to accept another she-slave for the use of the men, and she had proved skillful at doctoring, so they let her live. She had reddish hair, her voice was very soft, her name was Estrel. Beyond this he knew nothing about her; and she had not asked him anything at all about himself, not even his name.

He had escaped lightly, all things considered. Paristolis, the Noble Matter of ancient Cetian science, would not explode nor take fire, so the slider had not blown up under him, though its controls were wrecked. The bursting missile had chewed the left side of his head and upper body with fine shrapnel, but Estrel was there with the skill and a few of the materials of medicine. There was no infection; he recuperated fast, and within a few days of his blood-christening as Horressins he was planning escape with her.

But the days went on and no chances came. A defensive society: a wary, jealous people, all their actions rigidly scheduled by rite, custom, and tabu. Though each Hunter had his tent, women were held in common and all a man's doings were done with other men; they were less a community than a club or herd, interdependent members of one entity. In this effort to attain security, independence and privacy of course were suspect; Falk and Estrel had to snatch at any chance to talk for a moment. She did not know the Forest dialect, but they could use Galaktika, which the Basnasska spoke only in a pidgin form.

"The time to try," she said once, "might be during a snowstorm, when the snow would hide us and our tracks. But how far could we get on foot in a blizzard? You've got a compass; but the cold . . ."

Falk's wintercloth clothing had been confiscated, along with everything else he possessed, even the gold ring he had always worn. They had left him one gun: that was integral with his being a Hunter and could not be taken from him. But the clothes he had worn so long now covered the bony ribs and shanks of the Old Hunter Kessnokaty and he had his compass only because Estrel had got it and hidden it before they went through his pack. He and she were well enough clothed in Basnasska buckskin shirts and leggings, with boots and parkas of red cowhide; but nothing was adequate shelter from one of the prairie blizzards, with their hard subfreezing winds, except walls, roof and a fire.

"If we can get across into Samsit territory, just a few miles west of here, we could hole up in an Old Place I know there and hide till they give up looking. I thought of trying it before you came. But I had no compass and was afraid of getting lost in the storm. With a compass, and a gun, we might make it. . . . We might not."

"If it's our best chance," Falk said, "we'll take it."

He was not quite so naive, so hopeful and easily swayed, as he had been before his capture. He was a little more resistant and resolute. Though he had suffered at their hands he had no special grudge against the Basnasska; they had branded him once and for all down both his arms with the blue tattoo-slashes of their kinship, branding him as a barbarian, but also as a man. That was all right. But they had their business, and he had his. The hard individual will developed in him by his training in the Forest House demanded that he get free, that he get on with his journey, with what Zove had called *man's work*. These people were not going anywhere, nor did they come from anywhere, for they had cut their roots in the human past. It was not only the extreme precariousness of his existence among the Bas-

nasska that made him impatient to get out; it was also a
sense of suffocation, of being cramped and immobilized,
which was harder to endure than the bandage that
blanked his vision.

That evening Estrel stopped by his tent to tell him that
it had begun to snow, and they were settling their plan in
whispers when a voice spoke at the flap of the tent. Estrel
translated quietly: "He says, 'Blind Hunter, do you want
the Red Woman tonight?' " She added no explanation.
Falk knew the rules and etiquette of sharing the women
around; his mind was busy with the matter of their talk,
and he replied with the most useful of his short list of
Basnasska words—"Mieg!"—no.

The male voice said something more imperative. "If it
goes on snowing, tomorrow night, maybe," Estrel murmured in Galaktika. Still thinking, Falk did not answer.
Then he realized she had risen and gone, leaving him
alone in the tent. And after that he realized that she was
the Red Woman, and that the other man had wanted her
to copulate with.

He could simply have said Yes instead of No; and
when he thought of her cleverness and gentleness towards him, the softness of her touch and voice, and the
utter silence in which she hid her pride or shame, then he
winced at his failure to spare her, and felt himself humiliated as her fellowman, and as a man.

"We'll go tonight," he said to her next day in the drifted
snow beside the Women's Lodge. "Come to my tent.
Let a good part of the night pass first."

"Kokteky has told me to come to his tent tonight."

"Can you slip away?"

"Maybe."

"Which tent is Kokteky's?"

"Behind the Mzurra Society Lodge to the left. It has a patched place over the flap."

"If you don't come I'll come get you."

"Another night there might be less danger—"

"And less snow. Winter's getting on; this may be the last big storm. We'll go tonight."

"I'll come to your tent," she said with her unarguing, steady submissiveness.

He had left a slit in his bandage through which he could dimly see his way about, and he tried to see her now; but in the dull light she was only a gray shape in grayness.

In the late dark of that night she came, quiet as the windblown snow against the tent. They each had ready what they had to take. Neither spoke. Falk fastened his oxhide coat, pulled up and tied the hood, and bent to unseal the doorflap. He started aside as a man came pushing in from outside, bent double to clear the low gap—Kokteky, a burly shaven-headed Hunter, jealous of his status and his virility. "Horressins. The Red Woman—" he began, then saw her in the shadows across the embers of the fire. At the same moment he saw how she and Falk were dressed, and their intent. He backed up to close off the doorway or to escape from Falk's attack, and opened his mouth to shout. Without thought, reflex-quick and certain Falk fired his laser at pointblank range, and the brief flick of mortal light stopped the shout in the Basnassxa's mouth, burnt away mouth and brain and life in one moment, in perfect silence.

Falk reached across the embers, caught the woman's hand, and led her over the body of the man he had killed into the dark.

Fine snow on a light wind sifted and whirled, taking

73

their breaths with cold. Estrel breathed in sobs. His left hand holding her wrist and his right his gun, Falk set off west among the scattered tents, which were barely visible as slits and webs of dim orange. Within a couple of minutes even these were gone, and there was nothing at all in the world but night and snow.

Handlasers of Eastern Forest make had several settings and functions: the handle served as a lighter, and the weapon-tube converted to a not very efficient flashlight. Falk set his gun to give a glow by which they could read the compass and see the next few steps ahead, and they went on, guided by the mortal light.

On the long rise where the Basnasska winter-camp stood the wind had thinned the snowcover, but as they went on, unable to pick their course ahead, the compass West their one guideline in the confusion of the snowstorm that mixed air and ground into one whirling mess, they got onto lower land. There were four- and five-foot drifts through which Estrel struggled gasping like a spent swimmer in high seas. Falk pulled out the rawhide drawstring of his hood and tied it around his arm, giving her the end to hold, and then went ahead, making her a path. Once she fell and the tug on the line nearly pulled him down; he turned and had to seek for a moment with the light before he saw her crouching in his tracks, almost at his feet. He knelt, and in the wan, snowstreaked sphere of light saw her face for the first time clearly. She was whispering, "This is more than I bargained for. . . ."

"Get your breath a while. We're out of the wind in this hollow."

They crouched there together in a tiny bubble of light, around which hundreds of miles of wind-driven snow hurtled in darkness over the plains.

74

She whispered something which at first he did not understand: "Why did you kill the man?"

Relaxed, his senses dulled, drawing up resources of strength for the next stage of their slow, hard escape, Falk made no response. Finally with a kind of grin he muttered, "What else . . .?"

"I don't know. You had to."

Her face was white and drawn with strain; he paid no attention to what she said. She was too cold to rest there, and he got to his feet, pulling her up with him. "Come on. It can't be much farther to the river."

But it was much farther. She had come to his tent after some hours of darkness, as he thought of it—there was a word for *hours* in the Forest tongue, though its meaning was imprecise and qualitative, since a people without business and communication across time and space have no use for timepieces—and the winter night had still a long time to run. They went on, and the night went on.

As the first gray began to leaven the whirling black snowrubble of the storm they struggled down a slope of frozen tangled grass and shrubs. A mighty groaning bulk rose up straight in front of Falk and plunged off into the snow. Somewhere nearby they heard the snorting of another cow or bull, and then for a minute the great creatures were all about them, white muzzles and wild liquid eyes catching the light, the driven snow hillocky and bulking with flanks and shaggy shoulders. Then they were through the herd, and came down to the bank of the little river that separated Basnasska from Samsit territory. It was fast, shallow, unfrozen. They had to wade, the current tugging at their feet over loose stones, pulling at their knees, icily rising till they struggled waist-deep through burning cold. Estrel's legs gave way under her before they were clear across. Falk hauled her up out of the water and through the ice-crusted reedbeds of the west bank, and then again crouched down by her in blank exhaustion among the snowmounded bushes of the overhanging shore. He switched off his lightgun. Very faint, but very large, a stormy day was gaining on the dark.

"We have to go on, we've got to have a fire."

She did not reply.

He held her in his arms against him. Their boots and leggings and parkas from the shoulders down were frozen stiff already. The woman's face, bowed against his arm, was deathly white.

He spoke her name, trying to rouse her. "Estrel! Estrel, come on. We can't stay here. We can get on a little farther. It won't be so hard. Come on, wake up, little one, little hawk, wake up. . . ." In his great weariness he spoke to her as he had used to speak to Parth, at daybreak, a long time ago.

She obeyed him at last, struggling to her feet with his help, getting the line into her frozen gloves, and step by step following him across the shore, up the low bluffs, and on through the tireless, relentless, driving snow.

They kept along the rivercourse, going south, as she had told him they would do when they had planned their run. He had no real hope they could find anything in this spinning whiteness, as featureless as the night storm had been. But before long they came to a creek tributary to the river they had crossed, and turned up it, rough going for the land was broken. They struggled on. It seemed to Falk that by far the best thing to do would be to lie down and fall asleep, and he was only unable to do this

76

because there was someone who was counting
someone a long way off, a long time ago, who ha
him on a journey; he could not lie down, for he
accountable to someone. . . .

There was a croaking whisper in his ear, Estrel's voice.
Ahead of them a clump of high cottonwood boles loomed
like starving wraiths in the snow, and Estrel was tugging
at his arm. They began to stumble up and down the
north side of the snow-choked creek just beyond the cot-
tonwoods, searching for something. "A stone," she kept
saying, "a stone," and though he did not know why they
needed a stone, he searched and scrabbled in the snow
with her. They were both crawling on hands and knees
when at last she came on the landmark she was after, a
snowmounded block of stone a couple of feet high.

With her frozen gloves she pushed away the dry drifts
from the east side of the block. Incurious, listless with
fatigue, Falk helped her. Their scraping bared a metal
rectangle, level with the curiously level ground. Estrel
tried to open it. A hidden handle clicked, but the edges
of the rectangle were frozen shut. Falk spent his last
strength straining to lift the thing, till finally he came to
his wits and unsealed the frozen metal with the heatbeam
in the handle of his gun. Then they lifted up the door
and looked down a neat steep set of stairs, weirdly geo-
metric amidst this howling wilderness, to a shut door

"It's all right," his companion muttered, and going
down the stairs—crawling backwards, as on a ladder,
because she could not trust her legs—she pushed the
door open, and then looked up at Falk. "Come on!" she
said.

He came down, pulling the trapdoor to above him as
she directed. It was abruptly utterly dark, and crouching

on the steps Falk hastily pressed the stud of his handgun for light. Below him Estrel's white face glimmered. He came down and followed her in the door, into a place that was very dark and very big, so big his light could only hint at the ceiling and the nearer walls. It was silent, and the air was dead, flowing past them in a faint unchanging draft.

"There should be wood over here," Estrel's soft, strain-hoarsened voice said somewhere to his left. "Here. We need a fire; help me with this. . . ."

Dry wood was stacked in high piles in a corner near the entrance. While he got a blaze going, building it up inside a circle of blackened stones nearer the center of the cavern, Estrel crept off into some farther corner and returned dragging a couple of heavy blankets. They stripped and rubbed down, then huddled on the blankets, inside their Basnasska sleep-rolls, up close to the fire. It burned hot as if in a chimney, drawn up by a high draft that also carried off the smoke. There was no warming the great room or cave, but the firelight and heat relaxed and cheered them. Estrel got dried meat out of her bag, and they munched as they sat, though their lips were sore with frostbite and they were too tired to be hungry. Gradually the warmth of the fire began to soak into their bones.

"Who else has used this place?"

"Anyone that knows of it, I suppose."

"There was a mighty House here once, if this was the cellar," Falk said, looking into the shadows that flickered and thickened into impenetrable black at a distance from the fire, and thinking of the great basements under the house of Fear.

"They say there was a whole city here. It goes on a long way from the door, they say. I don't know."

"How did you know of it—are you a Samsit woman?"

"No."

He asked no further, recalling the code; but presently she said in her submissive way, "I am a Wanderer. We know many places like this, hiding places. . . . I suppose you've heard of the Wanderers."

"A little," said Falk, stretching out and looking across the fire at his companion. Tawny hair curled about her face as she sat huddled in the shapeless bag, and a pale jade amulet at her throat caught the firelight.

"They know little of us in the Forest."

"No Wanderers came as far east as my House. What was told of them there fits the Basnasska better—savages, hunters, nomads." He spoke sleepily, laying his head down on his arm.

"Some Wanderers might be called savages. Others not. The Cattle-Hunters are all savages and know nothing beyond their own territories, these Basnasska and Samsit and Arksa. We go far. We go east to the Forest, and south to the mouth of the Inland River, and west over the Great Mountains and the Western Mountains even to the sea. I myself have seen the sun set in the sea, behind the chain of blue isles that lies far off the coast, beyond the drowned valleys of California, earthquake-whelmed. . . ." Her soft voice had slipped into the cadence of some archaic chant or plaint. "Go on," Falk murmured, but she was still, and before long he was fast asleep. For a while she watched his sleeping face. At last she pushed the embers together, whispered a few words as if in prayer to the amulet chained around her neck, and curled down to sleep across the fire from him.

When he woke she was making a stand of bricks over the fire to support a kettle filled with snow. "It looks like late afternoon outside," she said, "but it could be morning, or noon for that matter. The storm's as thick as ever. They can't track us. And if they did, still they couldn't get in this place. . . . This kettle was in the cache with the blankets. And there's a bag of dried peas. We'll do well enough here." The hard, delicate face turned to him with a faint smile. "It's dark, though. I don't like the thick walls and the dark."

"It's better than bandaged eyes. Though you saved my life with that bandage. Blind Horressins was better off than dead Falk." He hesitated and then asked, "What moved you to save me?"

She shrugged, still with the faint, reluctant smile. "Fellow prisoners. . . . They always say Wanderers are clever at ruses and disguises. Did you not hear them call me Fox Woman? Let me look at those hurts of yours. I brought my bag of tricks."

"Are Wanderers all good healers, too?"

"We have certain skills."

"And you know the Old Tongue; you have not forgotten man's old way, like the Basnasska."

"Yes, we all know Galaktika. Look there, the rim of your ear was frostbitten yesterday. Because you took the tie from your hood for me to hold."

"I can't look at it," Falk said amiably, submitting to her doctoring. "I don't need to, usually."

As she dressed the still unhealed cut on his left temple she glanced once or twice sidelong at his face, and at last she ventured: "There are many Foresters with such eyes as yours, no doubt."

"None."

Evidently the code prevailed. She asked nothing, and he, having resolved to confide in no one, volunteered nothing. But his own curiosity got the better of him and he said, "They don't frighten you, then, these cat-eyes?"

"No," she answered in her quiet way. "You frightened me only once. When you shot—so fast—"

"He would have raised the whole camp."

"I know, I know. But we carry no guns. You shot so quick, I was frightened—it was like a terrible thing I saw once, when I was a child. A man who killed another with a gun, quicker than thought, like that. He was one of the Razes."

"Razes?"

"Oh, one meets with them in the Mountains sometimes."

"I know very little of the Mountains."

She explained, though as if unwillingly. "You know the Law of the Lords. They do not kill—you know. When there is a murderer in their city, they cannot kill him to stop him, so they make him into a Raze. It is something they do to the mind. They can turn him loose and he starts to live anew, innocent. This man I spoke of was older than you, but had a mind like a little child. But he got a gun in his hands, and his hands knew how to use it, and he—shot a man very close up, like you did—"

Falk was silent. He glanced across the fire at his handgun, lying atop his pack, the marvelous little tool that had started his fires, provided his meat, and lighted his darkness all his long way. There had been no knowledge in his hands of how to use the thing—had there? Metock had taught him how to shoot. He had learned from Metock, and grown skillful by hunting. He was sure of it. He could not be a mere freak and criminal given a second chance by the arrogant charity of the Lords of Es Toch. . . .

Yet was that not more plausible than his own vague dreams and notions of his origin?

"How do they do this to a man's mind?"

"I do not know."

"They might do it," he said harshly, "not only to criminals, but to—to rebels?"

"What are rebels?"

She spoke Galaktika much more fluently than he, but she had never heard that word.

She had finished dressing his hurt and was carefully tucking her few medicaments away in their pouch. He turned around to her so abruptly that she looked up startled, drawing back a little.

"Have you ever seen eyes like mine, Estrel?"

"No."

"You know—the City?"

"Es Toch? Yes, I have been there."

"Then you have seen the Shing?"

"You are no Shing."

"No. But I am going among them." He spoke fiercely. "But I dread—" He stopped.

Estrel closed the medicine-pouch and put it in her pack. "Es Toch is strange to men from the Lonely Houses and the far lands," she said at last in her soft, careful voice. "But I have walked its streets with no harm; many people live there, in no fear of the Lords. You need not go in dread. The Lords are very powerful, but much is told of Es Toch that is not true. . . ."

Her eyes met his. With sudden decision, summoning what paraverbal skill he had, he bespoke her for the first time: "Then tell me what is true of Es Toch!"

She shook her head, answering aloud, "I have saved your life and you mine, and we are companions, and fellow-Wanderers perhaps for a while. But I will not bespeak you or any person met by chance; not now, nor ever."

"Do you think me a Shing after all?" he asked ironically, a little humiliated, knowing she was right.

"Who can be sure?" she said, and then added with her faint smile, "Though I would find it hard to believe of you. . . . There, the snow in the kettle has melted down. I'll go up and get more. It takes so much to make a little water, and we are both thirsty. You . . . you are called Falk?"

He nodded, watching her.

"Don't mistrust me, Falk," she said. "Let me prove myself to you. Mindspeech proves nothing; and trust is a thing that must grow, from actions, across the days."

"Water it, then," said Falk, "and I hope it grows."

Later, in the long night and silence of the cavern, he roused from sleep to see her sitting hunched by the embers, her tawny head bowed on her knees. He spoke her name.

"I'm cold," she said. "There's no warmth left . . ."

"Come over to me." He spoke sleepily, smiling. She did not answer, but presently she came to him across the red-lit darkness, naked except for the pale jade stone between her breasts. She was slight, and shaking with the cold. In his mind which was in certain aspects that of a very young man he had resolved not to touch her, who had endured so much from the savages; but she murmured to him, "Make me warm, let me have solace." And he blazed up like fire in the wind, all resolution swept away by her

83

presence and her utter compliance. She lay all night in his arms, by the ashes of the fire.

Three more days and nights in the cavern, while the blizzard renewed and spent itself overhead, Falk and Estrel passed in sleep and lovemaking. She was always the same, yielding, acquiescent. He, having only the memory of the pleasant and joyful love he had shared with Parth, was bewildered by the insatiability and violence of the desire Estrel roused in him. Often the thought of Parth came to him accompanied by a vivid image, the memory of a spring of clear, quick water that rose among rocks in a shadowy place in the forest near the Clearing. But no memory quenched this thirst, and again he would seek satisfaction in Estrel's fathomless submissiveness and find, at least, exhaustion. Once it all turned to uncomprehended anger. He accused her; "You only take me because you think you have to, that I'd have raped you otherwise."

"And you would not?"

"No!" he said, believing it. "I don't want you to serve me, to obey me— Isn't it warmth, human warmth, we both want?"

"Yes," she whispered.

He would not come near her for a while; he resolved he would not touch her again. He went off by himself with his lightgun to explore the strange place they were in. After several hundred paces the cavern narrowed, becoming a high, wide, level tunnel. Black and still, it led him on perfectly straight for a long time, then turned without narrowing or branching and around the dark turning went on and on. His steps echoed dully. Nothing caught any brightness or cast any shadow from his light. He walked till he was weary and hungry, then turned. It was all the same, leading nowhere. He came back to Estrel, to the endless promise and unfulfillment of her embrace.

The storm was over. A night's rain had laid the black earth bare, and the last hollowed drifts of snow dripped and sparkled. Falk stood at the top of the stairway, sunlight on his hair, wind fresh on his face and in his lungs. He felt like a mole done hibernating, like a rat come out of a hole. "Let's go," he called to Estrel, and went back down to the cavern only to help her pack up quickly and clear out.

He had asked her if she knew where her people were, and she had answered, "Probably far ahead in the west, by now."

"Did they know you were crossing Basnasska territory alone?"

"Alone? It's only in fairytales from the Time of the Cities that women ever go anywhere alone. A man was with me. The Basnasska killed him." Her delicate face was set, unexpressive.

Falk began to explain to himself, then, her curious passivity, the want of response that had seemed almost a betrayal of his strong feeling. She had borne too much and could no longer respond. Who was the companion the Basnasska had killed? It was none of Falk's business to know, until she wanted to tell him. But his anger was gone and from that time on he treated Estrel with confidence and with tenderness.

"Can I help you look for your people?"

She said softly, "You are a kind man, Falk. But they will be far ahead, and I cannot comb all the Western Plains . . ."

The lost, patient note in her voice moved him. "Come

west with me, then, till you get news of them. You know what way I take."

It was still hard for him to say the name "Es Toch," which in the tongue of the Forest was an obscenity, abominable. He was not yet used to the way Estrel spoke of the Shing city as a mere place among other places.

She hesitated, but when he pressed her she agreed to come with him. That pleased him, because of his desire for her and his pity for her, because of the loneliness he had known and did not wish to know again. They set off together through the cold sunshine and the wind. Falk's heart was light at being outside, at being free, at going on. Today the end of the journey did not matter. The day was bright, the broad bright clouds sailed overhead, the way itself was its end. He went on, the gentle, docile, unwearying woman walking by his side.

V

THEY CROSSED the Great Plains on foot—which is soon said, but was not soon or easily done. The days were longer than the nights and the winds of spring were softening and growing mild when they first saw, even from afar, their goal: the barrier, paled by snow and distance, the wall across the continent from north to south. Falk stood still then, gazing at the Mountains.

"High in the mountains lies Es Toch," Estrel said, gazing with him. "There I hope we each shall find what we seek."

"I often fear it more than I hope it. . . . Yet I'm glad to have seen the mountains."

"We should go on from here."

"I'll ask the Prince if he is willing that we go tomorrow."

But before leaving her he turned and looked eastward at the desert land beyond the Prince's gardens a while, as if looking back across all the way he and she had come together.

He knew still better now how empty and mysterious a world men inhabited in these later days of their history. For days on end he and his companion had gone and never seen one trace of human presence.

Early in their journey they had gone cautiously, through the territories of the Samsit and other Cattle-Hunter nations, which Estrel knew to be as predatory as the Basnasska. Then, coming to more arid country, they were forced to keep to ways which others had used before, in order to find water; still, when there were signs of people having recently passed, or living nearby, Estrel kept a sharp lookout, and sometimes changed their course to avoid even the risk of being seen. She had a general, and in places a remarkably specific, knowledge of the vast area they were crossing; and sometimes when the terrain worsened and they were in doubt which direction to take, she would say, "Wait till dawn," and going a little away would pray a minute to her amulet, then come back, roll up in her sleepingbag and sleep serenely: and the way she chose at dawn was always the right one. "Wanderer's instinct," she said when Falk admired her guessing. "Anyway, so long as we keep near water and far from human beings, we are safe."

But once, many days west of the cavern, following the curve of a deep stream-valley they came so abruptly upon a settlement that the guards of the place were around them before they could run. Heavy rain had hidden any sight or sound of the place before they reached it. When the people offered no violence and proved willing to take them in for a day or two, Falk was glad of it, for walking and camping in that rain had been a miserable business.

This tribe or people called themselves the Bee-Keepers.

A strange lot, literate and laser-armed, all clothed alike, men and women, in long shifts of yellow wintercloth marked with a brown cross on the breast, they were hospitable and uncommunicative. They gave the travelers beds in their barrack-houses, long, low, flimsy buildings of wood and clay, and plentiful food at their common table; but they spoke so little, to the strangers and among themselves, that they seemed almost a community of the dumb. "They're sworn to silence. They have vows and oaths and rites, no one knows what it's all about," Estrel said, with the calm uninterested disdain which she seemed to feel for most kinds of men. The Wanderers must be proud people, Falk thought. But the Bee-Keepers went her scorn one better: they never spoke to her at all. They would talk to Falk, "Does your she want a pair of our shoes?" —as if she were his horse and they had noticed she wanted shoeing. Their own women used male names, and were addressed and referred to as men. Grave girls, with clear eyes and silent lips, they lived and worked as men among the equally grave and sober youths and men. Few of the Bee-Keepers were over forty and none were under twelve. It was a strange community, like the winter barracks of some army encamped here in the midst of utter solitude in the truce of some unexplained war; strange, sad, and admirable. The order and frugality of their living reminded Falk of his Forest home, and the sense of a hidden but flawless, integral dedication was curiously restful to him. They were so sure, these beautiful sexless warriors, though what they were so sure of they never told the stranger.

"They recruit by breeding captured savage women like sows, and bringing up the brats in groups. They worship something called the Dead God, and placate him with sacrifice—murder. They are nothing but the vestige of some ancient superstition," Estrel said, when Falk had said something in favor of the Bee-Keepers to her. For all her submissiveness she apparently resented being treated as a creature of a lower species. Arrogance in one so passive both touched and entertained Falk, and he teased her a little:

"Well, I've seen you at nightfall mumbling to your amulet. Religions differ. . . ."

"Indeed they do," she said, but she looked subdued.

"Who are they armed against, I wonder?"

"Their Enemy, no doubt. As if they could fight the Shing. As if the Shing need bother to fight them!"

"You want to go on, don't you?"

"Yes. I don't trust these people. They keep too much hidden."

That evening he went to take his leave of the head of the community, a gray-eyed man called Hiardan, younger perhaps than himself. Hiardan received his thanks laconically, and then said in the plain, measured way the Bee-Keepers had, "I think you have spoken only truth to us. For this I thank you. We would have welcomed you more freely and spoken to you of things known to us, if you had come alone."

Falk hesitated before he answered. "I am sorry for that. But I would not have got this far but for my guide and friend. And . . . you live here all together, Master Hiardan. Have you ever been alone?"

"Seldom," said the other. "Solitude is soul's death: man is mankind. So our saying goes. But also we say, do not put your trust in any but brother and hive-twin, known since infancy. That is our rule. It is the only safe one."

"But I have no kinsmen, and no safety, Master," Falk

said, and bowing soldierly in the Bee-Keepers' fashion, he took his leave, and next morning at daybreak went on westward with Estrel.

From time to time as they went they saw other settlements or encampments, none large, all wide-scattered—five or six of them perhaps in three or four hundred miles. At some of these Falk left to himself would have stopped. He was armed, and they looked harmless: a couple of nomad tents by an ice-rimmed creek, or a little solitary herdboy on a great hillside watching the half-wild red oxen, or, away off across the rolling land, a mere feather of bluish smoke beneath the illimitable gray sky. He had left the Forest to seek, as it were, some news of himself, some hint of what he was or guide towards what he had been in the years he could not remember; how was he to learn if he dared not risk asking? But Estrel was afraid to stop even at the tiniest and poorest of these prairie settlements. "They do not like Wanderers," she said, "nor any strangers. Those that live so much alone are full of fear. In their fear they would take us in and give us food and shelter. But then in the night they would come and bind and kill us. You cannot go to them, Falk"—and she glanced at his eyes—"and tell them *I am your fellow-man.* . . . They know we are here; they watch. If they see us move on tomorrow they won't trouble us. But if we don't move on, or if we try to go to them, they'll fear us. It is fear that kills."

Windburned and travelweary, his hood pushed back so the keen, glowing wind from the red west stirred his hair, Falk sat, arms across his knees, near their campfire in the lee of a knobbed hill. "True enough," he said, though he spoke wistfully, his gaze on that far-off wisp of smoke. "Perhaps that's the reason why the Shing kill no one."

91

Estrel knew his mood and was trying to hearten him, to change his thoughts.

"Why's that?" he asked, aware of her intent, but unresponsive.

"Because they are not afraid."

"Maybe." She had got him to thinking, though not very cheerfully. Eventually he said, "Well, since it seems I must go straight to them to ask my questions, if they kill me I'll have the satisfaction of knowing that I frightened them. . . ."

Estrel shook her head. "They will not. They do not kill."

"Not even cockroaches?" he inquired, venting the ill-temper of his weariness on her. "What do they do with cockroaches, in their City—disinfect them and set them free again, like the Razes you told me about?"

"I don't know," Estrel said; she always took his questions seriously. "But their law is reverence for life, and they do keep the law."

"They don't revere human life. Why should they?— they're not human."

"But that is why their rule is reverence for all life—isn't it? And I was taught that there have been no wars on Earth or among the worlds since the Shing came. It is humans that murder one another!"

"There are no humans that could do to me what the Shing did. I honor life, I honor it because it's a much more difficult and uncertain matter than death; and the most difficult and uncertain quality of all is intelligence. The Shing kept their law and let me live, but they killed my intelligence. Is that not murder? They killed the man I was, the child I had been. To play with a man's mind so,

is that reverence? Their law is a lie, and their reverence is
mockery."

Abashed by his anger, Estrel knelt by the fire cutting
up and skewering a rabbit he had shot. The dusty reddish hair curled close to her bowed head; her face was
patient and remote. As ever, she drew him to her by
compunction and desire. Close as they were, yet he never
understood her; were all women so? She was like a lost
room in a great house, like a carven box to which he did
not have the key. She kept nothing from him and yet her
secrecy remained, untouched.

Enormous evening darkened over rain-drenched miles
of earth and grass. The little flames of their fire burned
red-gold in the clear blue dusk.

"It's ready, Falk," said the soft voice.

He rose and came to her beside the fire. "My friend,
my love," he said, taking her hand a moment. They sat
down side by side and shared their meat, and later their
sleep.

As they went farther west the prairies began to grow
dryer, the air clearer. Estrel guided them southward for
several days in order to avoid an area which she said was,
or had been, the territory of a very wild nomad people,
the Horsemen. Falk trusted her judgment, having no
wish to repeat his experience with the Basnasska. On the
fifth and sixth day of this southward course they crossed
through a hilly region and came into dry, high terrain,
flat and treeless, forever windswept. The gullies filled
with torrents during the rain, and next day were dry
again. In summer this must be semidesert; even in spring
it was very dreary.

As they went on they twice passed ancient ruins, mere
mounds and hummocks, but aligned in the spacious

geometry of streets and squares. Fragments of pottery, flecks of colored glass and plastic were thick in the spongy ground around these places. It had been two or three thousand years, perhaps, since they had been inhabited. This vast steppe-land, good only for cattle-grazing, had never been resettled after the diaspora to the stars, the date of which in the fragmentary and falsified records left to men was not definitely known.

"Strange to think," Falk said as they skirted the second of these long-buried towns, "that there were children playing here and . . . women hanging out the washing . . . so long ago. In another age. Farther away from us than the worlds around a distant star."

"The Age of Cities," Estrel said, "the Age of War. . . . I never heard tell of these places, from any of my people. We may have come too far south, and be heading for the Deserts of the South."

So they changed course, going west and a little north, and the next morning came to a big river, orange and turbulent, not deep but dangerous to cross, though they spent the whole day seeking a ford.

On the western side, the country was more arid than ever. They had filled their flasks at the river, and as water had been a problem by excess rather than default, Falk thought little about it. The sky was clear now, and the sun shone all day; for the first time in hundreds of miles they did not have to resist the cold wind as they walked, and could sleep dry and warm. Spring came quick and radiant to the dry land; the morning star burned above the dawn and wildflowers bloomed under their steps. But they did not come to any stream or spring for three days after crossing the river.

In their struggle through the flood Estrel had taken

some kind of chill. She said nothing about it, but she did not keep up her untiring pace, and her face began to look wan. Then dysentery attacked her. They made camp early. As she lay beside their brushwood fire in the evening she began to cry, a couple of dry sobs only, but that was much for one who kept emotion so locked within herself.

Uneasy, Falk tried to comfort her, taking her hands; she was hot with fever.

"Don't touch me," she said. "Don't, don't. I lost it, I lost it, what shall I do?"

And he saw then that the cord and amulet of pale jade were gone from her neck.

"I must have lost it crossing the river," she said controlling herself, letting him take her hand.

"Why didn't you tell me—"

"What good?"

He had no answer to that. She was quiet again, but he felt her repressed, feverish anxiety. She grew worse in the night and by morning was very ill. She could not eat, and though tormented by thirst could not stomach the rabbit-blood which was all he could offer her to drink. He made her as comfortable as he could and then taking their empty flasks set off to find water.

Mile after mile of wiry, flower-speckled grass and clumped scrub stretched off, slightly rolling, to the bright hazy edge of the sky. The sun shone very warm; desert larks went up singing from the earth. Falk went at a fast steady pace, confident at first, then dogged, quartering out a long sweep north and east of their camp. Last week's rains had already soaked deep into this soil, and there were no streams. There was no water. He must go on and seek west of the camp. Circling back from the east he was looking out anxiously for the camp when, from a long low rise, he saw something miles off to westward, a smudge, a dark blur that might be trees. A moment later he spotted the nearer smoke of the campfire, and set off towards it at a jogging run, though he was tired, and the low sun hammered its light in his eyes, and his mouth was dry as chalk.

Estrel had kept the fire smoldering to guide him back. She lay by it in her worn-out sleepingbag. She did not lift her head when he came to her.

"There are trees not too far to the west of here; there may be water. I went the wrong way this morning," he said, getting their things together and slipping on his pack. He had to help Estrel get to her feet; he took her arm and they set off. Bent, with a blind look on her face, she struggled along beside him for a mile and then for another mile. They came up one of the long swells of land. "There!" Falk said; "there—see it? It's trees, all right—there must be water there."

But Estrel had dropped to her knees, then lain down on her side in the grass, doubled up on her pain, her eyes shut. She could not walk farther.

"It's two or three miles at most, I think. I'll make a smudge-fire here, and you can rest; I'll go fill the flasks and come back— I'm sure there's water there, and it won't take long." She lay still while he gathered all the scrub-wood he could and made a little fire and heaped up more of the green wood where she could put it on the fire. "I'll be back soon," he said, and started away. At that she sat up, white and shivering, and cried out, "No! don't leave me! You mustn't leave me alone—you mustn't go—"

There was no reasoning with her. She was sick and frightened beyond the reach of reason. Falk could not leave her there, with the night coming; he might have, but it did not seem to him that he could. He pulled her up, her arm over his shoulder, half pulling and half carrying her, and went on.

On the next rise he came in sight of the trees again, seeming no nearer. The sun was setting away off ahead of them in a golden haze over the ocean of land. He was carrying Estrel now, and every few minutes he had to stop and lay his burden down and drop down beside her to get breath and strength. It seemed to him that if he only had a little water, just enough to wet his mouth, it would not be so hard.

"There's a house," he whispered to her, his voice dry and whistling. Then again, "It's a house, among the trees. Not much farther. . . ." This time she heard him, and twisted her body feebly and struggled against him, moaning, "Don't go there. No, don't go there. Not to the houses. Ramarren mustn't go to the houses. Falk—" She took to crying out weakly in a tongue he did not know, as if crying for help. He plodded on, bent down under her weight.

Through the late dusk light shone out sudden and golden in his eyes: light shining through high windows, behind high dark trees.

A harsh, howling noise rose up, in the direction of the light, and grew louder, coming closer to him. He struggled on, then stopped, seeing shadows running at him out of the dusk, making that howling, coughing clamor. Heavy shadow-shapes as high as his waist encircled him, lunging and snapping at him where he stood supporting Estrel's unconscious weight. He could not draw his gun and dared not move. The lights of the high windows shone serenely, only a few hundred yards away. He shouted, "Help us! Help!" but his voice was only a croaking whisper.

Other voices spoke aloud, calling sharply from a distance. The dark shadow-beasts withdrew, waiting. People came to him where, still holding Estrel against him, he had dropped to his knees. "Take the woman," a man's voice said; another said clearly, "What have we here?—a new pair of toolmen?" They commanded him to get up, but he resisted, whispering, "Don't hurt her—she's sick—"

"Come on, then!" Rough and expeditious hands forced him to obey. He let them take Estrel from him. He was so dizzy with fatigue that he made no sense of what happened to him and where he was until a good while had passed. They gave him his fill of cool water, that was all he knew, all that mattered.

He was sitting down. Somebody whose speech he could not understand was trying to get him to drink a glassful of some liquid. He took the glass and drank. It was stinging stuff, strongly scented with juniper. A glass—a little glass of slightly clouded green: he saw that clearly, first. He had not drunk from a glass since he had left Zove's House. He shook his head, feeling the volatile liquor clear his throat and brain, and looked up.

He was in a room, a very large room. A long expanse of polished stone floor vaguely mirrored the farther wall, on which or in which a great disk of light glowed soft yellow. Radiant warmth from the disk was palpable on his lifted face. Halfway between him and the sunlike circle of light a tall, massive chair stood on the bare floor; beside it, unmoving, silhouetted, a dark beast crouched.

"What are you?"

He saw the angle of nose and jaw; the black hand on

the arm of the chair. The voice was deep, and hard as stone. The words were not in the Galaktika he had now spoken for so long but in his own tongue, the Forest speech, though a different dialect of it. He answered slowly with the truth.

"I do not know what I am. My self-knowledge was taken from me six years ago. In a Forest House I learned the way of man. I go to Es Toch to try to learn my name and nature."

"You go to the Place of the Lie to find out the truth? Tools and fools run over weary Earth on many errands, but that beats all for folly or a lie. What brought you to my Kingdom?"

"My companion—"

"Will you tell me that she brought you here?"

"She fell sick; I was seeking water. Is she—"

"Hold your tongue. I am glad you did not say she brought you here. Do you know this place?"

"No."

"This is the Kansas Enclave. I am its master. I am its lord, its Prince and God. I am in charge of what happens here. Here we play one of the great games. King of the Castle it's called. The rules are very old, and are the only laws that bind me. I make the rest."

The soft tame sun glowed from floor to ceiling and from wall to wall behind the speaker as he rose from his chair. Overhead, far up, dark vaults and beams held the unflickering golden light reflected among shadows. The radiance silhouetted a hawk nose, a high slanting forehead, a tall, powerful, thin frame, majestic in posture, abrupt in motion. As Falk moved a little the mythological beast beside the throne stretched and snarled. The juniper-scented liquor had volatilized his thoughts; he should be thinking that madness caused this man to call himself a king, but was thinking rather that kingship had driven this man mad.

"You have not learned your name, then?"

"They called me Falk, those who took me in."

"To go in search of his true name: what better way has a man ever gone? No wonder it brought you past my gate. I take you as a Player of the Game," said the Prince of Kansas. "Not every night does a man with eyes like yellow jewels come begging at my door. To refuse him would be cautious and ungracious, and what is royalty but risk and grace? They called you Falk, but I do not. In the game you are the Opalstone. You are free to move. Griffon, be still!"

"Prince, my companion—"

"—is a Shing or a tool or a woman: what do you keep her for? Be still, man; don't be so quick to answer kings. I know what you keep her for. But she has no name and does not play in the game. My cowboys' women are looking after her, and I will not speak of her again." The Prince was approaching him, striding slowly across the bare floor as he spoke. "My companion's name is Griffon. Did you ever hear in the old Canons and Legends of the animal called dog? Griffon is a dog. As you see, he has little in common with the yellow yappers that run the plains, though they are kin. His breed is extinct, like royalty. Opalstone, what do you most wish for?"

The Prince asked this with shrewd, abrupt geniality, looking into Falk's face. Tired and confused and bent on speaking truth, Falk answered: "To go home."

"To go home. . . ." The Prince of Kansas was black as his silhouette or his shadow, an old, jetblack man seven feet tall with a face like a swordblade. "To go home. . . ." He had moved away a little to study the long table near Falk's chair. All the top of the table, Falk now saw, was sunk several inches into a frame, and contained a network of gold and silver wires upon which beads were strung, so pierced that they could slip from wire to wire and, at certain points, from level to level. There were hundreds of beads, from the size of a baby's fist to the size of an apple seed, made of clay and rock and wood and metal and bone and plastic and glass and amethyst, agate, topaz, turquoise, opal, amber, beryl, crystal, garnet, emerald, diamond. It was a patterning-frame, such as Zove and Buckeye and others of the House possessed. Thought to have come originally from the great culture of Davenant, though it was now very ancient on Earth, the thing was a fortune-teller, a computer, an implement of mystical discipline, a toy. In Falk's short second life he had not had time to learn much about patterning-frames. Buckeye had once remarked that it took forty or fifty years to get handy with one; and hers, handed down from old in her family, had been only ten inches square, with twenty or thirty beads. . . .

A crystal prism struck an iron sphere with a clear, tiny clink. Turquoise shot to the left and a double link of polished bone set with garnets looped off to the right and down, while a fire-opal blazed for a moment in the dead center of the frame. Black, lean, strong hands flashed over the wires, playing with the jewels of life and death. "So," said the Prince, "you want to go home. But look! Can you read the frame? Vastness. Ebony and diamond and crystal, all the jewels of fire: and the Opal-stone among them, going on, going out. Farther than the

King's House, farther than the Wallwindow Prison, farther than the hills and hollows of Kopernik, the stone flies among the stars. Will you break the frame, time's frame? See there!"

The slide and flicker of the bright beads blurred in Falk's eyes. He held to the edge of the great patterning-frame and whispered, "I cannot read it. . . ."

"This is the game you play, Opalstone, whether you can read it or not. Good, very good. My dogs have barked at a beggar tonight and he proves a prince of starlight. Opalstone, when I come asking water from your wells and shelter within your walls, will you let me in? It will be a colder night than this. . . . And a long time from now! You come from very, very long ago. I am old but you are much older; you should have died a century ago. Will you remember a century from now that in the desert you met a King? Go on, go on, I told you you are free to move here. There are people to serve you if you need them."

Falk found his way across the long room to a curtained portal. Outside it in an anteroom a boy waited; he summoned others. Without surprise or servility, deferent only in that they waited for Falk to speak first, they provided him a bath, a change of clothing, supper, and a clean bed in a quiet room.

Thirteen days in all he lived in the Great House of the Enclave of Kansas, while the last light snow and the scattered rains of spring drove across the desert lands beyond the Prince's gardens. Estrel, recovering, was kept in one of the many lesser houses that clustered behind the great one. He was free to be with her when he chose . . . free to do anything he chose. The Prince ruled his domain absolutely, but in no way was his rule enforced: rather it was accepted as an honor; his people chose to serve him, perhaps because they found, in thus affirming the innate and essential grandeur of one person, that they reaffirmed their own quality as men. There were not more than two hundred of them, cowboys, gardeners, makers and menders, their wives and children. It was a very little kingdom. Yet to Falk, after a few days, there was no doubt that had there been no subjects at all, had he lived there quite alone, the Prince of Kansas would have been no more and no less a prince. It was, again, a matter of quality.

This curious reality, this singular validity of the Prince's domain, so fascinated and absorbed him that for days he scarcely thought of the world outside, that scattered, violent, incoherent world he had been traveling through so long. But talking on the thirteenth day with Estrel and having spoken of going, he began to wonder at the relation of the Enclave with all the rest, and said, "I thought the Shing suffered no lordship among men. Why should they let him guard his boundaries here, calling himself Prince and King?"

"Why should they not let him rave? This Enclave of Kansas is a great territory, but barren and without people. Why should the Lords of Es Toch interfere with him? I suppose to them he is like a silly child, boasting and babbling.

"Is he that to you?"

"Well—did you see when the ship came over, yesterday?"

"Yes, I saw."

An aircar—the first Falk had ever seen, though he had

recognized its throbbing drone—had crossed directly over the house, up very high so that it was in sight for some minutes. The people of the Prince's household had run out into the gardens beating pans and clappers, the dogs and children had howled, the Prince on an upper balcony had solemnly fired off a series of deafening firecrackers, until the ship had vanished in the murky west.

"They are as foolish as the Basnasska, and the old man is mad."

Though the Prince would not see her, his people had been very kind to her; the undertone of bitterness in her soft voice surprised Falk. "The Basnasska have forgotten the old way of man," he said; "these people maybe remember it too well." He laughed. "Anyway, the ship did go on over."

"Not because they scared it away with firecrackers, Falk," she said seriously, as if trying to warn him of something.

He looked at her a moment. She evidently saw nothing of the lunatic, poetic dignity of those firecrackers, which ennobled even a Shing aircar with the quality of a solar eclipse. In the shadow of total calamity why not set off a firecracker? But since her illness and the loss of her jade talisman she had been anxious and joyless, and the sojourn here which pleased Falk so was a trial to her. It was time they left. "I shall go speak to the Prince of our going," he told her gently, and leaving her there under the willows, now beaded yellowgreen with leaf-buds, he walked up through the gardens to the great house. Five of the long-legged, heavy-shouldered black dogs trotted along with him, an honor guard he would miss when he left this place.

The Prince of Kansas was in his throne-room, reading. The disk that covered the east wall of the room by day shone cool mottled silver, a domestic moon; only at night did it glow with soft solar warmth and light. The throne, of polished petrified wood from the southern deserts, stood in front of it. Only on the first night had Falk seen the Prince seated on the throne. He sat now in one of the chairs near the patterning-frame, and at his back the twenty-foot-high windows looking to the west were uncurtained. There the far, dark mountains stood, tipped with ice.

The Prince raised his swordblade face and heard what Falk had to say. Instead of answering he touched the book he had been reading, not one of the beautiful decorated projector-scrolls of his extraordinary library but a little handwritten book of bound paper. "Do you know this Canon?"

Falk looked where he pointed and saw the verse,

> What men fear
> must be feared.
> O desolation!
> It has not yet
> not yet reached its limit!

"I know it, Prince. I set out on this journey of mine with it in my pack. But I cannot read the page to the left, in your copy."

"Those are the symbols it was first written in, five or six thousand years ago: the tongue of the Yellow Emperor—my ancestor. You lost yours along the way? Take this one, then. But you'll lose it too, I expect; in following the

Way the way is lost. O desolation! Why do you always speak the truth, Opalstone?"

"I'm not sure." In fact, though Falk had gradually determined that he would not lie no matter whom he spoke to or how chancy the truth might seem, he did not know why he had come to this decision. "To—to use the enemy's weapon is to play the enemy's game. . . ."

"Oh, they won their game long ago. —So you're off? Go on, then; no doubt it's time. But I shall keep your companion here a while."

"I told her I would help her find her people, Prince."

"Her people?" The hard, shadowy face turned to him. "What do you take her for?"

"She is a Wanderer."

"And I am a green walnut, and you a fish, and those mountains are made of roasted sheepshit! Have it your way. Speak the truth and hear the truth. Gather the fruits of my flowery orchards as you walk westward, Opalstone, and drink the milk of my thousand wells in the shade of giant ferntrees. Do I not rule a pleasant kingdom? Mirages and dust straight west to the dark. Is it lust or loyalty that makes you hold to her?"

"We have come a long way together."

"Mistrust her!"

"She has given me help, and hope; we are companions. There is trust between us—how can I break it?"

"Oh fool, oh desolation!" said the Prince of Kansas. "I'll give you ten women to accompany you to the Place of the Lie, with lutes and flutes and tambourines and contraceptive pills. I'll give you five good friends armed with firecrackers. I'll give you a dog—in truth I will, a living extinct dog, to be your true companion. Do you know why dogs died out? Because they were loyal, because they were trusting. Go alone, man!"

"I cannot."

"Go as you please. The game here's done." The Prince rose, went to the throne beneath the moon-circle, and seated himself. He never turned his head when Falk tried to say farewell.

VI

WITH HIS lone memory of a lone peak to embody the word "mountain," Falk had imagined that as soon as they reached the mountains they would have reached Es Toch; he had not realized they would have to clamber over the roof-tree of a continent. Range behind range the mountains rose; day after day the two crept upward into the world of the heights, and still their goal lay farther up and farther on to the southwest. Among the forests and torrents and the cloud-conversant slopes of snow and granite there was every now and then a little camp or village along the way. Often they could not avoid these as there was but one path to take. They rode past on their mules, the Prince's princely gift at their going, and were not hindered. Estrel said that the mountain people, living here on the doorstep of the Shing, were a wary lot who would neither molest nor welcome a stranger, and were best left alone.

Camping was a cold business, in April in the mountains, and the once they stopped at a village was a welcome relief. It was a tiny place, four wooden houses by a noisy stream in a canyon shadowed by great· storm-wreathed peaks; but it had a name, Besdio, and Estrel had stayed there once years ago, she told him, when she had been a girl. The people of Besdio, a couple of whom were light-skinned and tawny-haired like Estrel herself, spoke with her briefly. They talked in the language which the Wanderers used; Falk had always spoken Galaktika with Estrel and had not learned this Western tongue. Estrel explained, pointing east and west; the mountain people nodded coolly, studying Estrel carefully, glancing at Falk only out of the corner of their eyes. They asked few questions, and gave food and a night's shelter un-grudgingly but with a cool, incurious manner that made Falk vaguely uneasy.

The cowshed where they were to sleep was warm, however, with the live heat of the cattle and goats and poultry crowded there in sighing, odorous, peaceable companionship. While Estrel talked a little longer with their hosts in the main hut, Falk betook himself to the cowshed and made himself at home. In the hayloft above the stalls he made a luxurious double bed of hay and spread their bedrolls on it. When Estrel came he was already half asleep, but he roused himself enough to re-mark, "I'm glad you came . . . I smell something kept hidden here, but I don't know what."

"It's not all I smell."

This was as close as Estrel had ever come to making a joke, and Falk looked at her with a bit of surprise. "You are happy to be getting close to the City, aren't you?" he asked. "I wish I were."

"Why shouldn't I be? There I hope to find my kinsfolk; if I do not, the Lords will help me. And there you will find what you seek too, and be restored into your heritage."

"My heritage? I thought you thought me a Raze."

"You? Never! Surely you don't believe, Falk, that it was the Shing that meddled with your mind? You said that once, down on the plains, and I did not understand you then. How could you think yourself a Raze, or any common man? You are not Earthborn!"

Seldom had she spoken so positively. What she said heartened him, concurring with his own hope, but her saying it puzzled him a little, for she had been silent and troubled for a long time now. Then he saw something swing from a leather cord around her neck: "They gave you an amulet." That was the source of her hopefulness.

"Yes," she said, looking down at the pendant with satisfaction. "We are of the same faith. Now all will go well for us."

He smiled a little at her superstition, but was glad it gave her comfort. As he went to sleep he knew she was awake, lying looking into the darkness full of the stink and the gentle breath and presence of the animals. When the cock crowed before daylight he half-roused and heard her whispering prayers to her amulet in the tongue he did not know.

They went on, taking a path that wound south of the stormy peaks. One great mountain bulwark remained to cross, and for four days they climbed, till the air grew thin and icy, the sky dark blue, and the sun of April shone dazzling on the fleecy backs of clouds that grazed the meadows far beneath their way. Then, the summit of the pass attained, the sky darkened and snow fell on the naked rocks and blanked out the great bare slopes of red and gray. There was a hut for wayfarers in the pass, and they and their mules huddled in it till the snow stopped and they could begin the descent.

"Now the way is easy," Estrel said, turning to look at Falk over her mule's jogging rump and his mule's nodding ears; and he smiled, but there was a dread in him that only grew as they went on and down, towards Es Toch.

Closer and closer they came, and the path widened into a road; they saw huts, farms, houses. They saw few people, for it was cold and rainy, keeping people indoors under a roof. The two wayfarers jogged on down the lonely road through the rain. The third morning from the summit dawned bright, and after they had ridden a couple of hours Falk halted his mule, looking questioningly at Estrel.

"What is it, Falk?"

"We have come—this is Es Toch, isn't it?"

The land had leveled out all about them, though distant peaks closed the horizon all around, and the pastures and plowlands they had been riding through had given way to houses, houses and still more houses. There were huts, cabins, shanties, tenements, inns, shops where goods were made and bartered for, children everywhere, people on the highway, people on side-roads, people afoot, on horses and mules and sliders, coming and going: it was crowded yet scanty, slack and busy, dirty, dreary and vivid under the bright dark sky of morning in the mountains.

"It is a mile or more yet to Es Toch."

"Then what is this city?"

"This is the outskirts of the city."

Falk stared about him, dismayed and excited. The road he had followed so far from the house in the Eastern

111

Forest had become a street, leading only too quickly to its end. As they sat their mules in the middle of the street people glanced at them, but none stayed and none spoke. The women kept their faces averted. Only some of the ragged children stared, or pointed shouting and then ran, vanishing up a filth-encumbered alley or behind a shack. It was not what Falk had expected; yet what had he expected? "I did not know there were so many people in the world," he said at last. "They swarm about the Shing like flies on dung."

"Fly-maggots flourish in dung," Estrel said dryly. Then, glancing at him, she reached across and put her hand lightly on his. "These are the outcasts and the hangers-on, the rabble outside the walls. Let us go on to the city, the true City. We have come a long way to see it. . . ."

They rode on; and soon they saw, jutting up over the shanty roofs, the walls of windowless green towers, bright in the sunlight.

Falk's heart beat hard; and he noticed that Estrel spoke a moment to the amulet she had been given in Besdio.

"We cannot ride the mules inside the city," she said. "We can leave them here." They stopped at a ramshackle public stable; Estrel talked persuasively a while in the Western tongue with the man who kept the place, and when Falk asked what she had been asking him she said, "To keep our mules as surety."

"Surety?"

"If we don't pay for their keep, he will keep them. You have no money, have you?"

"No," Falk said humbly. Not only did he have no money, he had never seen money; and though Galaktika had a word for the thing, his Forest dialect did not.

The stable was the last building on the edge of a field of rubble and refuse which separated the shantytown from a high, long wall of granite blocks. There was one entrance to Es Toch for people on foot. Great conical pillars marked the gate. On the left-hand pillar an inscription in Galaktika was carved: REVERENCE FOR LIFE. On the right was a longer sentence in characters Falk had never seen. There was no traffic through the gate, and no guard.

"The pillar of the Lie and the pillar of the Secret," he said aloud as he walked between them, refusing to let himself be overawed; but then he entered Es Toch, and saw it, and stood still saying nothing.

The City of the Lords of Earth was built on the two rims of a canyon, a tremendous cleft through the mountains, narrow, fantastic, its black walls striped with green plunging terrifically down half a mile to the silver tinsel strip of a river in the shadowy depths. On the very edges of the facing cliffs the towers of the city jutted up, hardly based on earth at all, linked across the chasm by delicate bridgespans. Towers, roadways and bridges ceased and the wall closed the city off again just before a vertiginous bend of the canyon. Helicopters with diaphanous vanes skimmed the abyss, and sliders flickered along the half-glimpsed streets and slender bridges. The sun, still not far above the massive peaks to eastward, seemed scarcely to cast shadows here; the great green towers shone as if translucent to the light.

"Come," Estrel said, a pace ahead of him, her eyes shining. "There's nothing to fear here, Falk."

He followed her. There was no one on the street, which descended between lower buildings toward the cliff-edge towers. Once he glanced back at the gate, but he could no longer see the opening between the pillars.

"Where do we go?"

"There's a place I know, a house where my people come." She took his arm, the first time she had ever done so in all the way they had walked together, and clinging to him kept her eyes lowered as they came down the long zigzag street. Now to their right the buildings loomed up high as they neared the city's heart, and to the left, without wall or parapet, the dizzy gorge dropped away full of shadows, a black gap between the luminous perching towers.

"But if we need money here—"

"They'll look after us."

People brightly and strangely dressed passed them on sliders; the landing-ledges high up the sheer-walled buildings flickered with helicopters. High over the gorge an aircar droned, going up.

"Are these all . . . Shing?"

"Some."

Unconsciously he was keeping his free hand on his laser. Estrel without looking at him, but smiling a little, said, "Do not use your lightgun here, Falk. You came here to gain your memory, not to lose it."

"Where are we going, Estrel?"

"Here."

"This? This is a palace."

The luminous greenish wall towered up windowless, featureless, into the sky. Before them a square doorway stood open.

"They know me here. Don't be afraid. Come on with me."

She clung to his arm. He hesitated. Looking back up

114

the street he saw several men, the first he had seen on foot, loitering towards them, watching them. That scared him, and with Estrel he entered the building, passing through inner automatic portals that slid apart at their approach. Just inside, possessed by a sense of misjudgment, having made a hideous error, he stopped. "What is this place? Estrel—"

It was a high hall, full of a thick greenish light, dim as an underwater cave; there were doorways and corridors, down which men approached, hurrying towards him. Estrel had broken away from him. In panic he turned to the doors behind him: they were shut now. They had no handles. Dim figures of men broke into the hall, running at him and shouting. He backed up against the shut doors and reached for his laser. It was gone. It was in Estrel's hands. She stood behind the men as they surrounded Falk, and as he tried to break through them and was seized, and fought and was beaten, he heard for a moment a sound he had never heard before: her laugh.

A disagreeable sound rang in Falk's ears; a metallic taste filled his mouth. His head swam when he raised it, and his eyes would not focus, and he could not seem to move freely. Presently he realized that he was waking from unconsciousness, and thought he could not move because he had been hurt or drugged. Then he made out that his wrists were shackled together on a short chain, his ankles likewise. But the swimming in his head grew worse. There was a great voice booming in his ears now, repeating the same thing over and over: *ramarren-ramarren-ramarren*. He struggled and cried out, trying to get away from the booming voice which filled him with terror. Lights flashed in his eyes, and through the sound roaring in his head he heard someone scream in his own voice, "I am not—"

When he came to again everything was utterly still. His head ached, and still he could not see very clearly; but there were no shackles on his arms and legs now, if there ever had been any, and he knew he was being protected, sheltered, looked after. They knew who he was and he was welcome. His own people were coming for him, he was safe here, cherished, beloved, and all he need do now was rest and sleep, rest and sleep, while the soft, deep stillness murmured tenderly in his head, *marren-marren-marren*. . . .

He woke. It took a while, but he woke, and managed to sit up. He had to bury his acutely aching head in his arms for a while to get over the vertigo the movement caused, and at first was aware only that he was sitting on the floor of some room, a floor which seemed to be warm and yielding, almost soft, like the flank of some great beast. Then he lifted his head, and got his eyes into focus, and looked about him.

He was alone, in the midst of a room so uncanny that it revived his dizziness for a while. There was no furniture. Walls floor and ceiling were all of the same translucent stuff, which appeared soft and undulant like many thicknesses of pale green veiling, but was tough and slick to the touch. Queer carvings and crimpings and ridges forming ornate patterns all over the floor were, to the exploring hand, nonexistent; they were eye-deceiving paintings, or lay beneath a smooth transparent surface. The angles were walls met were thrown out of true by optical-illusion devices of crosshatching and pseudo-parallels used as decoration; to pull the corners into right angles took an effort of will, which was perhaps an effort of self-deception, since they might, after all, not be right angles. But none of this teasing subtlety of decoration so disoriented Falk as the fact that the entire room was translucent. Vaguely, with the effect of looking into a depth of very green pond-water, underneath him another room was visible. Overhead was a patch of light that might be the moon, blurred and greened by one or more intervening ceilings. Through one wall of the room strings and patches of brightness were fairly distinct, and he could make out the motion of the lights of helicopters or aircars. Through the other three walls these outdoor lights were much dimmer, blurred by the veilings of further walls, corridors, rooms. Shapes moved in those other rooms. He could see them but there was no identifying them: features, dress, color, size, all was blurred away. A blot of shadow somewhere in the green depths suddenly rose and grew less, greener, dimmer, fading into the maze of vagueness. Visibility without discrimination, solitude without privacy. It was extraordinarily beautiful, this masked shimmer of lights and shapes through inchoate planes of green, and extraordinarily disturbing.

All at once in a brighter patch on the near wall Falk caught a glimpse of movement. He turned quickly and with a shock of fear saw something at last vivid, distinct: a face, a seamed, savage, staring face set with two inhuman yellow eyes.

"A Shing," he whispered in blank dread. The face mocked him, the terrible lips mouthing soundlessly *A Shing*, and he saw that it was the reflection of his own face.

He got up stiffly and went to the mirror and passed his hand over it to make sure. It was a mirror, half concealed

117

by a molded frame painted to appear flatter than it actually was.

He turned from it at the sound of a voice. Across the room from him, not too clear in the dim, even light from hidden sources, but solid enough, a figure stood. There was no doorway visible, but a man had entered, and stood looking at him: a very tall man, a white cape or cloak dropping from wide shoulders, white hair, clear, dark, penetrating eyes. The man spoke; his voice was deep and very gentle. "You are welcome here, Falk. We have long awaited you, long guided and guarded you." The light was growing brighter in the room, a clear, swelling radiance. The deep voice held a note of exaltation. "Put away fear and be welcome among us, O Messenger. The dark road is behind you and your feet are set upon the way that leads you home!" The brilliance grew till it dazzled Falk's eyes; he had to blink and blink again, and when he looked up, squinting, the man was gone.

There came unbidden into his mind words spoken months ago by an old man in the Forest: *The awful darkness of the bright lights of Es Toch.*

He would not be played with, drugged, deluded any longer. A fool he had been to come here, and he would never get away alive; but he would not be played with. He started forward to find the hidden doorway to follow the man. A voice from the mirror said, "Wait a moment more, Falk. Illusions are not always lies. You seek truth."

A seam in the wall split and opened into a door; two figures entered. One, slight and small, strode in; he wore breeches fitted with an ostentatious codpiece, a jerkin, a close-fitting cap. The second, taller, was heavily robed and moved mincingly, posing like a dancer; long, purplish-black hair streamed down to her waist—his waist,

118

it must be for the voice though very soft was deep. "We are being filmed, you know, Strella."

"I know," said the little man in Estrel's voice. Neither of them so much as glanced at Falk; they behaved as if they were alone. "Go on with what you were about to say, Kradgy."

"I was about to ask you why it took you so long."

"So long? You are unjust, my Lord. How could I track him in the Forest east of Shorg?—it is utter wilderness. The stupid animals were no help; all they do these days is babble the Law. When you finally dropped me the man-finder I was two hundred miles north of him. When I finally caught up he was heading straight into Basnasska territory. You know the Council has them furnished with bombirds and such so that they can thin out the Wanderers and the Solia-pachim. So I had to join the filthy tribe. Have you not heard my reports? I sent them in all along, till I lost my sender crossing a river south of Kansas Enclave. And my mother in Besdio gave me another. Surely they kept my reports on tape?"

"I never listen to reports. In any case, it was all time and risk wasted, since you did not in all these weeks succeed in teaching him not to fear us."

"Estrel," Falk said. "Estrel!"

Grotesque and frail in her transvestite clothes, Estrel did not turn, did not hear. She went on speaking to the robed man. Choked with shame and anger Falk shouted her name, then strode forward and seized her shoulder—and there was nothing there, a blur of lights in the air, a flicker of color, fading.

The door-slit in the wall still stood open, and through it Falk could see into the next room. There stood the robed man and Estrel, their backs to him. He said her name in a whisper, and she turned and looked at him. She looked into his eyes without triumph and without shame, calmly, passively, detached and uncaring, as she had looked at him all along.

"Why—why did you lie to me?" he said. "Why did you bring me here?" He knew why; he knew what he was and always had been in Estrel's eyes. It was not his intelligence that spoke, but his self-respect and his loyalty, which could not endure or admit the truth in this first moment.

"I was sent to bring you here. You wanted to come here."

He tried to pull himself together. Standing rigid, not moving towards her, he asked, "Are you a Shing?"

"I am," said the robed man, affably smiling. "I am a Shing. All Shing are liars. Am I, then, a Shing lying to you, in which case of course I am not a Shing, but a non-Shing, lying? Or is it a lie that all Shing lie? But I am a Shing, truly; and truly I lie. Terrans and other animals have been known to tell lies also; lizards change color, bugs mimic sticks and flounders lie by lying still, looking pebbly or sandy depending on the bottom which underlies them. Strella, this one is even stupider than the child."

"No, my Lord Kradgy, he is very intelligent," Estrel replied, in her soft, passive way. She spoke of Falk as a human being speaks of an animal.

She had walked beside Falk, eaten with him, slept with him. She had slept in his arms. . . . Falk stood watching her, silent; and she and the tall one also stood silent, unmoving, as if awaiting a signal from him to go on with their performance.

He could not feel rancor towards her. He felt nothing

towards her. She had turned to air, to a blur and flicker of light. His feeling was all towards himself: he was sick, physically sick, with humiliation.

Go alone, Opalstone, said the Prince of Kansas. Go alone, said Hiardan the Bee-Keeper. Go alone, said the old Listener in the forest. Go alone, my son, said Zove. How many others would have guided him aright, helped him on his quest, armed him with knowledge, if he had come across the prairies alone? How much might he have learned, if he had not trusted Estrel's guidance and good faith?

Now he knew nothing, except that he had been measurelessly stupid, and that she had lied. She had lied to him from the start, steadily, from the moment she told him she was a Wanderer—no, from before that: from the moment she had first seen him and had pretended not to know who or what he was. She had known all along, and had been sent to make sure he got to Es Toch; and to counteract, perhaps, the influence those who hated the Shing had had and might have upon his mind. But then why, he thought painfully, standing there, in one room gazing at her in another, why had she stopped lying, now?

"It does not matter what I say to you now," she said, as if she had read his thoughts.

Possibly she had. They had never used mindspeech; but if she was a Shing and had the mental powers of the Shing, the extent of which was only a matter of rumor and speculation among men, she might have been attuned to his thoughts all along, all the weeks of their traveling. How could he tell? There was no use asking her. . . .

There was a sound behind him. He turned, and saw

two people standing at the other end of the room, near the mirror. They wore black gowns and white hoods, and were twice the height of ordinary men.

"You are too easily fooled," said one giant.

"You must know you have been fooled," said the other. "You are half a man only."

"Half a man cannot know the whole truth."

"He who hates is mocked and fooled."

"He who kills is razed and tooled."

"Where do you come from, Falk?"

"What are you, Falk?"

"Where are you, Falk?"

"Who are you, Falk?"

Both giants raised their hoods, showing that there was nothing inside but shadow, and backed into the wall, and through it, and vanished.

Estrel ran to him from the other room, flung her arms about him, pressing herself against him, kissing him hungrily, desperately. "I love you, I have loved you since I first saw you. Trust me, Falk, trust me!" Then she was torn from him, wailing, "Trust me!" and was drawn away as if pulled by some mighty, invisible force, as if blown by a great wind, whirled about, blown through a slit doorway that closed silently behind her, like a mouth closing.

"You realize," said the tall male in the other room, "that you are under the influence of hallucinatory drugs." His whispering, precise voice held an undertone of sarcasm and ennui. "Trust yourself least of all. Eh?" He then lifted his long robes and urinated copiously; after which he wandered out, rearranging his robes and smoothing his long flowing hair.

Falk stood watching the greenish floor of the other room gradually absorb the urine till it was quite gone.

The sides of the door were very slowly drawing together, closing the slit. It was the only way out of the room in which he was trapped. He broke from his lethargy and ran through the slit before it shut. The room in which Estrel and the other one had stood was exactly the same as the one he had left, perhaps a trifle smaller and dimmer. A slit-door stood open in its far wall, but was closing very slowly. He hurried across the room and through it, and into a third room which was exactly like the others, perhaps a trifle smaller and dimmer. The slit in its far wall was closing very slowly, and he hurried through it into another room, smaller and dimmer than the last, and from it squeezed through into another small, dim room, and from it crawled into a small dim mirror and fell upwards, screaming in sick terror, towards the white, seamed, staring moon.

He woke, feeling rested, vigorous, and confused, in a comfortable bed in a bright, windowless room. He sat up, and as if that had given a signal two men came hurrying from behind a partition, big men with a staring, bovine look to them. "Greetings Lord Agad! Greetings Lord Agad!" they said one after the other, and then, "Come with us, please, come with us, please." Falk stood up, stark naked, ready to fight—the only thing clear in his mind at the moment was his fight and defeat in the entrance hall of the palace—but they offered no violence. "Come on, please," they repeated antiphonally, until he came with them. They led him, still naked, out of the room, up a long blank corridor, through a mirror-walled hall, up a staircase that turned out to be a ramp painted to look like stairs, through another corridor and up more ramps, and finally into a spacious, furnished room with bluish-green walls, one of which was glowing with sunlight. One of the men stopped outside the room; the other entered with Falk. "There's clothes, there's food, there's drink. Now you—now you eat, drink. Now you— now you ask for need. All right?" He stared persistently but without any particular interest at Falk.

There was a pitcher of water on the table, and the first thing Falk did was drink his fill, for he was very thirsty. He looked around the strange, pleasant room with its furniture of heavy, glass-clear plastic and its windowless, translucent walls, and then studied his guard or attendant with curiosity. A big, blank-faced man, with a gun strapped to his belt. "What is the Law?" he asked on impulse.

Obediently and with no surprise the big, staring fellow answered, "Do not take life."

"But you carry a gun."

"Oh, this gun, it makes you all stiff, not dead," said the guard, and laughed. The modulations of his voice were arbitrary, not connected with the meaning of the words, and there was a slight pause between the words and the laugh. "Now you eat, drink, get clean. Here's good clothes. See, here's clothes."

"Are you a Raze?"

"No. I am a Captain of the Bodyguard of the True Lords, and I key in to the Number Eight computer. Now you eat, drink, get clean."

"I will if you leave the room."

A slight pause. "Oh yes, very well, Lord Agad," said the big man, and again laughed as if he had been tickled. Perhaps it tickled when the computer spoke through his brain. He withdrew. Falk could see the vague hulking shapes of the two guards through the inner wall of the room; they waited one on either side of the door in the corridor. He found the washroom and washed up. Clean clothes were laid out on the great soft bed that filled one end of the room; they were loose long robes patterned wildly with red, magenta and violet, and he examined them with distaste, but put them on. His battered backpack lay on the table of gold-mounted glassy plastic, its contents seemingly untouched, but his clothes and guns were not in evidence. A meal was laid out, and he was hungry. How long had it been since he had entered the doors that closed behind him? He had no idea, but his hunger told him it had been some while, and he fell to. The food was queer stuff, highly flavored, mixed, sauced, and disguised, but he ate it all and looked for more. There being no more, and since he had done what he had been asked to do, he examined the room more carefully. He could not see the vague shadows of the guards on the other side of the semi-transparent, bluish-green wall any longer, and was going to investigate when he stopped short. The barely visible vertical slit of the door was widening, and a shadow moved behind it. It opened to a tall oval, through which a person stepped into the room.

A girl, Falk thought at first, then saw it was a boy of sixteen or so, dressed in loose robes like those he wore himself. The boy did not come close to Falk, but stopped, holding out his hands palm upwards, and spouted a whole rush of gibberish.

"Who are you?"

"Orry," said the young man, "Orry!" and more gibberish. He looked frail and excited; his voice shook with emotion. He then dropped down on both knees and bowed his head low, a bodily gesture that Falk had never seen, though its meaning was unmistakable: it was the full and original gesture, of which, among the Bee-Keepers and the subjects of the Prince of Kansas, he had seen certain vestigial remnants.

"Speak in Galaktika," Falk said fiercely, shocked and uneasy. "Who are you?"

"I am Har-Orry-Prech-Ramarren," the boy whispered.

"Get up. Get off your knees. I don't— Do you know me?"

"Prech Ramarren, do you not remember me? I am Orry, Har Weden's son—"

"What is my name?"

The boy raised his head, and Falk stared at him—at his eyes, which looked straight into his own. They were of a gray-amber color, except for the large dark pupil: all iris, without visible white, like the eyes of a cat or a stag, like no eyes Falk had ever seen, except in the mirror last night.

"Your name is Agad Ramarren," the boy said, frightened and subdued.

"How do you know it?"

"I—I have always known it, prech Ramarren."

"Are you of my race? Are we of the same people?"

"I am Har Weden's son, prech Ramarren! I swear to you I am!"

There were tears in the gray-old eyes for a moment. Falk himself had always tended to react to stress with a brief blinding of tears; Buckeye had once reproved him for being embarrassed by this trait, saying it appeared to be a purely physiological reaction, probably racial.

The confusion, bewilderment, disorientation Falk had undergone since he had entered Es Toch now left him

126

unequipped to question and judge this latest apparition. Part of his mind said, *That is exactly what they want: they want you confused to the point of total credulity.* At this point he did not know whether Estrel—Estrel whom he knew so well and loved so loyally—was a friend or a Shing or a tool of the Shing, whether she had ever told him the truth or ever lied to him, whether she had been trapped here with him or had lured him here into a trap. He remembered a laugh; he also remembered a desperate embrace, a whisper. . . . What then was he to make of this boy, this boy looking at him in awe and pain with unearthly eyes like his own: would he turn if touched to a blur of lights? Would he answer questions with lies, or truth?

Amidst all illusions, errors and deceptions there remained, it seemed to Falk, only one way to take: the way he had followed all along, from Zove's House on. He looked at the boy again and told him the truth.

"I do not know you. If I should remember you, I do not, because I remember nothing longer ago than four or five years." He cleared his throat, turned away again, sat down on one of the tall spindly chairs, motioned for the boy to do the same.

"You . . . do not remember Werel?"

"Who is Werel?"

"Our home. Our world."

That hurt. Falk said nothing.

"Do you remember the—the journey here, prech Ramarren?" the boy asked, stammering. There was incredulity in his voice; he seemed not to have taken in what Falk had told him. There was also a shaken, yearning note, checked by respect or fear.

Falk shook his head.

Orry repeated his question with a slight change: "You do remember our journey to Earth, prech Ramarren?"

"No. When was the journey?"

"Six Terran years ago. —Forgive me, please, prech Ramarren. I did not know—I was over by the California Sea and they sent an aircar for me, an automatic; it did not say what I was wanted for. Then Lord Kradgy told me one of the Expedition had been found, and I thought —But he did not tell me this about your memory— You remember . . . only . . . only the Earth, then?"

He seemed to be pleading for a denial. "I remember only the Earth," Falk said, determined not to be swayed by the boy's emotion, or his naiveté, or the childish candor of his face and voice. He must assume that this Orry was not what he seemed to be.

But if he was?

I will not be fooled again, Falk thought bitterly.

Yes you will, another part of his mind retorted; *you will be fooled if they want to fool you, and there is no way you can prevent it. If you ask no questions of this boy lest the answer be a lie, then the lie prevails entirely, and nothing comes of all your journey here but silence and mockery and disgust. You came to learn your name. He gives you a name: accept it.*

"Will you tell me who . . . who we are?"

The boy eagerly began again in his gibberish, then checked himself at Falk's uncomprehending gaze. "You don't remember how to speak Kelshak, prech Ramarren?" He was almost plaintive.

Falk shook his head. "Kelshak is your native language?"

The boy said, "Yes," adding timidly, "And yours, prech Ramarren."

128

"What is the word for 'father' in Kelshak?"

"Hiowech. Or wawa—for babies." A flicker of an ingenuous grin passed over Orry's face.

"What would you call an old man whom you respected?"

"There are a lot of words like that—kinship words—Prevwa, kioinap, ska n-gehoy . . . Let me think, prechna. I haven't spoken Kelshak for so long. . . . A prechnoweg —a higher-level non-relative could be tiokioi, or previotio—"

"Tiokioi. I said the word once, not . . . knowing where I learned it. . . ."

It was no real test. There was no test here. He had never told Estrel much about his stay with the old Listener in the Forest, but they might have learned every memory in his brain, everything he had ever said or done or thought, while he was drugged in their hands this past night or nights. There was no knowing what they had done; there was no knowing what they could do, or would. Least of all could he know what they wanted. All he could do was go ahead trying to get at what he wanted.

"Are you free to come and go here?"

"Oh, yes, prech Ramarren. The Lords have been very kind. They have long been seeking for any . . . other survivors of the Expedition. Do you know, prechna, if any of the others . . ."

"I do not know."

"All that Kradgy had time to tell me, when I got here a few minutes ago, was that you had been living in the forest in the eastern part of this continent, with some wild tribe."

"I'll tell you of that if you want to know. But tell me

somethings first. I do not know who I am, who you are, what the Expedition was, what Werel is."

"We are Kelshy," the boy said with constraint, evidently embarrassed at explaining on so low a level to one he considered his superior, in age of course, but also in more than age. "Of the Kelshak Nation, on Werel—we came here on the ship *Alterra*—"

"Why did we come here?" Falk asked, leaning forward.

And slowly, with digressions and backtrackings and a thousand question-interruptions, Orry went on, till he was worn out with talking and Falk with hearing, and the veil-like walls of the room were glowing with evening light; then they were silent for a while, and dumb servants brought in food and drink for them. And all the time he ate and drank Falk kept gazing in his mind at the jewel that might be false and might be priceless, the story, the pattern, the glimpse—true vision or not—of the world he had lost.

VII

A SUN LIKE a dragon's eye, orange-yellow, like a fire-opal with seven glittering pendants swinging slowly through their long ellipses. The green third planet took sixty of Earth's years to complete its year: *Lucky the man who sees his second spring*, Orry translated a proverb of that world. The winters of the northern hemisphere, tilted by the angle of the ecliptic away from the sun while the planet was at its farthest from the sun, were cold, dark, terrible: the vast summers, half a lifetime long, were measurelessly opulent. Giant tides of the planet's deep seas obeyed a giant moon that took four hundred days to wax and wane; the world was rife with earthquakes, volcanoes, plants that walked, animals that sang, men who spoke and built cities: a catalogue of wonders. To this miraculous though not unusual world had come, twenty years ago, a ship from outer space. Twenty of its great years, Orry meant: something over twelve hundred Terran years.

Colonists and hilfers of the League of All Worlds, the

people on that ship were committing their work and lives to the new-found planet, remote from the ancient central worlds of the League, in the hope of bringing its native intelligent species eventually into the League, a new ally in the War To Come. Such had been the policy of the League ever since, generations before, warnings had come from beyond the Hyades of a great wave of conquerors that moved from world to world, from century to century, closer toward the farflung cluster of eighty planets that so proudly called itself the League of All Worlds. Terra, near the edge of the League heart-zone and the nearest League planet to the new-found planet Werel, had supplied all the colonists on this first ship. There were to have been other ships from other worlds of the League, but none ever came: the War came first.

The colonists' only communications with Earth, with the Prime World Davenant, and the rest of the League, was by the ansible, the instantaneous transmitter, aboard their ship. No ship, said Orry, had ever flown faster than light—here Falk corrected him. Warships had indeed been built on the ansible principle, but they had been only automatic death-machines, incredibly costly and carrying no living creatures. Lightspeed, with its foreshortening of time for the voyager, was the limit of human voyaging, then and now. So the colonists of Werel were a very long way from home and wholly dependent on their ansible for news. They had only been on Werel five years when they were informed that the Enemy had come, and immediately after that the communications grew confused, contradictory, intermittent, and soon ceased altogether. About a third of the colonists chose to take the ship and fly back across the great gap of years to Earth, to rejoin their people. The rest stayed on Werel, self-marooned. In their lifetimes they could never know what had become of their home world and the League they served, or who the Enemy was, and whether he ruled the League or had been vanquished. Without ship or communicator, isolated, they stayed, a small colony surrounded by curious and hostile High Intelligence Life Forms of a culture inferior, but an intelligence equal, to their own. And they waited, and their sons' sons waited, while the stars stayed silent over them. No ship ever came, no word. Their own ship must have been destroyed, the records of the new planet lost. Among all the stars the little orange-yellow opal was forgotten.

The colony thrived, spreading up a pleasant sea-coast land from its first town, which was named Alterra. Then after several years—Orry stopped and corrected himself, "Nearly six centuries, Earth-style, I mean. It was the Tenth Year of the Colony, I think. I was just beginning to learn history; but Father and . . . and you, prech Ramarren, used to tell me these things, before we made the Voyage, to explain it all to me . . ." After several centuries, then, the colony had come onto hard days. Few children were conceived, still fewer born alive. Here again the boy paused, explaining finally, "I remember your telling me that the Alterrans didn't know what was happening to them, they thought it was some bad effect of inbreeding, but actually it was a sort of selection. The Lords, here, say it couldn't have been that, that no matter how long an alien colony is established on a planet they remain alien. With gene-manipulation they can breed with natives, but the children will always be sterile. So I don't know what it was that happened to the Alterrans— I was only a child when you and Father were trying to tell me the story—I do remember you spoke of selection towards a . . . viable type . . . Anyhow, the colonists were getting near extinction when what was left of them finally managed to make an alliance with a native Werelian nation, Tevar. They wintered-through together, and when the Spring breeding season came, they found that Tevarans and Alterrans could reproduce. Enough of them, at least, to found a hybrid race. The Lords say that is not possible. But I remember you telling it to me." The boy looked worried and a little vague.

"Are we descendants of that race?"

"You are descended from the Alterra Agat, who led the colony through the Winter of the Tenth Year! We learned about Agat even in boy-school. That is your name, prech Ramarren—Agad of Charen. I am of no such lineage, but my great-grandmother was of the family Esmy of Kiow—that is an Alterran name. Of course, in a democratic society as Earth's, these distinctions are meaningless, aren't they . . . ?" Again Orry looked worried, as if some vague conflict was occurring in his mind. Falk steered him back to the history of Werel, filling out with guesses and extrapolation the childish narrative that was all Orry could supply.

The new mixed stock and mixed culture of the Tevar-Alterran nation flourished in the years after that perilous Tenth Winter. The little cities grew; a mercantile culture was established on the single north-hemisphere continent. Within a few generations it was spreading to the primitive peoples of the southern continents, where the problem of keeping alive through the winter was more easily solved. Population went up; science and technology began their exponential climb, guided and aided always by the Books of Alterra, the ship's library, the mysteries of which grew explicable as the colonists' remote descendants relearned lost knowledge. They had kept and copied those books, generation after generation, and learned the tongue they were written in—Galaktika, of course. Finally, the moon and sister-planets all explored, the sprawl of cities and the rivalries of nations controlled and balanced by the powerful Kelshak Empire in the old Northland, at the height of an age of peace and vigor the Empire had built and sent forth a lightspeed ship.

That ship, the *Alterra*, left Werel eighteen and a half years after the ship of the Colony from Earth landed: twelve hundred years, Earth style. Its crew had no idea what they would find on Earth. Werel had not yet been able to reconstruct the principles of the ansible transmitter, and had hesitated to broadcast radio-signals that would betray their location to a possible hostile world ruled by the Enemy the League had feared. To get information living men must go, and return, crossing the long night to the ancient home of the Alterrans.

"How long was that voyage?"

"Over two Werelian years—maybe a hundred and thirty or forty light-years— I was only a boy, a child, prech Ramarren, and some things I didn't understand, and much wasn't told me—"

Falk did not see why this ignorance should embarrass the lad; he was much more struck by the fact that Orry, who looked fifteen or sixteen, had been alive for perhaps a hundred and fifty years. And himself?

The *Alterra*, Orry went on, had left from a base near the old coast-town Tevar, her coordinates set for Terra. She had carried nineteen people, men, women and children, Kelshak for the most part and claiming Colonist descent: the adults selected by the Harmonious Council of the Empire for training, intelligence, courage, generosity, and arlesh.

"I don't know a word for it in Galaktika. It's just arlesh." Orry smiled his ingenuous smile. "Rale is . . . the right thing to do, like learning things at school, or like a river following its course, and arlesh derives from rale, I guess."

"Tao?" asked Falk; but Orry had never heard of the Old Canon of Man.

"What happened to the ship? What happened to the other seventeen people?"

"We were attacked at the Barrier. The Shing got there only after the *Alterra* was destroyed and the attackers were dispersing. They were rebels, in planetary cars. The Shing rescued me off one. They didn't know whether the rest of us had been killed or carried off by the rebels. They kept searching, over the whole planet, and about a year ago they heard a rumor about a man living in the Eastern Forest—that sounded like it might be one of us . . ."

"What do you remember of all this—the attack and so on?"

"Nothing. You know how lightspeed flight affects you—"

"I know that for those in the ship, no time passes. But I have no idea how that feels."

"Well, I don't really remember it very clearly. I was just a boy—nine years old, Earth style. And I'm not sure anybody could remember it clearly. You can't tell how—how things relate. You see and hear, but it doesn't hang together—nothing *means* anything—I can't explain it. It's horrible, but only like a dream. But then coming down into planetary space again, you go through what the

Lords call the Barrier, and that blacks out the passengers, unless they're prepared for it. Our ship wasn't. None of us had come to when we were attacked, and so I don't remember it, any—any more than you, prech Ramarren. When I came to I was aboard a Shing vessel."

"Why were you brought along as a boy?"

"My father was the captain of the expedition. My mother was on the ship too. You know, otherwise, prech Ramarren—well, if one came back one's people would all have been dead, long long ago. Not that it mattered—my parents are dead, now, anyhow. Or maybe they were treated like you, and . . . and wouldn't recognize me if we met. . . ."

"What was my part in the expedition?"

"You were our navigator."

The irony of that made Falk wince, but Orry went on in his respectful, naive fashion, "Of course, that means you set the ship's course, the coordinates—you were the greatest prosteny, a mathematician-astronomer, in all Kelshy. You were prechnowa to all of us aboard except my father, Har Weden. You are of the Eighth Order, prech Ramarren! You—you remember something of that—?"

Falk shook his head.

The boy subsided, saying at last, sadly, "I can't really believe that you don't remember, except when you do that."

"Shake my head?"

"On Werel we shrug for no. This way."

Orry's simplicity was irresistible. Falk tried the shrug; and it seemed to him that he found a certain rightness in it, a propriety, that could persuade him that it was indeed an old habit. He smiled, and Orry at once cheered up. "You are so like yourself, prech Ramarren, and so different! Forgive me. But what did they do, what did they do to make you forget so much?"

"They destroyed me. Surely I'm like myself. I am myself. I'm Falk. . . ." He put his head in his hands. Orry, abashed, was silent. The quiet, cool air of the room glowed like a blue-green jewel around them; the western wall was lambent with late sunlight.

"How closely do they watch you here?"

"The Lords like me to carry a communicator if I go off by aircar." Orry touched the bracelet on his left wrist, which appeared to be simple gold links. "It can be dangerous, after all, among the natives."

"But you're free to go where you like?"

"Yes, of course. This room of yours is just like mine, across the canyon." Orry looked puzzled again. "We have no enemies here, you know, prech Ramarren," he ventured.

"No? Where are our enemies, then?"

"Well—outside—where you came from—"

They stared at each other in mutual miscomprehension.

"You think men are our enemies—Terrans, human beings? You think it was they that destroyed my mind?"

"Who else?" Orry said, frightened, gaping.

"The aliens—the Enemy—the Shing!"

"But," the boy said with timid gentleness, as if realizing at last how utterly his former lord and teacher was ignorant and astray, "there never was an Enemy. There never was a War."

The room trembled softly like a tapped gong to an almost sub-aural vibration, and a moment afterward a voice, disembodied, spoke: *The Council meets.* The slit-door parted and a tall figure entered, stately in white robes and an ornate black wig. The eyebrows were shaven and repainted high; the face, masked by makeup to a matte smoothness, was that of a husky man of middle age. Orry rose quickly from the table and bowed, whispering, "Lord Abundibot."

"Har Orry," the man acknowledged, his voice also damped to a creaking whisper, then turned to Falk. "Agad Ramarren. Be welcome. The Council of Earth meets, to answer your questions and consider your requests. Behold now . . ." He had glanced at Falk only for a second, and did not approach either Werelian closely. There was a queer air about him of power and also of utter self-containment, self-absorption. He was apart, unapproachable. All three of them stood motionless a moment; and Falk, following the others' gaze, saw that the inner wall of the room had blurred and changed, seeming to be now a depth of clear grayish jelly in which lines and forms twitched and flickered. Then the image came clear, and Falk caught his breath. It was Estrel's face, ten times lifesize. The eyes gazed at him with the remote composure of a painting.

"I am Strella Siobelbel." The lips of the image moved, but the voice had no locality, a cold, abstract whisper trembling in the air of the room. "I was sent to bring to the City in safety the member of the Werel Expedition said to be living in the East of Continent One. I believe this to be the man."

And her face, fading, was replaced by Falk's own.

A disembodied voice, sibilant, inquired, "Does Har Orry recognize this person?"

As Orry answered, his face appeared on the screen.

139

"This is Agad Ramarren, Lords, the Navigator of the *Alterra*."

The boy's face faded and the screen remained blank, quivering, while many voices whispered and rustled in the air, like a brief multitudinous discussion among spirits, speaking an unknown tongue. This was how the Shing held their Council: each in his own room, apart, with only the presence of whispering voices. As the incomprehensible questioning and replying went on, Falk murmured to Orry, "Do you know this tongue?"

"No, prech Ramarren. They always speak Galaktika to me."

"Why do they talk this way, instead of face to face?"

"There are so many of them—thousands and thousands meet in the Council of Earth, Lord Abundibot told me. And they are scattered over the planet in many places, though Es Toch is the only city. That is Ken Kenyek, now."

The buzz of disembodied voices had died away and a new face had appeared on the screen, a man's face, with dead white skin, black hair, pale eyes. "Agad Ramarren, we are met in Council, and you have been brought into our Council, that you may complete your mission to Earth and, if you desire, return to your home. The Lord Pelleu Abundibot will bespeak you."

The wall abruptly blanked, returned to its normal translucent green. The tall man across the room was gazing steadily at Falk. His lips did not move, but Falk heard him speak, not in a whisper now but clearly— singularly clearly. He could not believe it was mind-speech, yet it could be nothing else. Stripped of the character and timbre, the incarnateness of voice, this was comprehensibility pure and simple, reason addressing reason.

"We mindspeak so that you may hear only truth. For it is not true that we who call ourselves Shing, or any other man, can pervert or conceal truth in paraverbal speech. The Lie that men ascribe to us is itself a lie. But if you choose to use voicespeech do so, and we will do likewise."

"I have no skill at bespeaking," Falk said aloud after a pause. His living voice sounded loud and coarse after the brilliant, silent mind-contact. "But I hear you well enough. I do not ask for the truth. Who am I to demand the truth? But I should like to hear what you choose to tell me."

Young Orry looked shocked. Abundibot's face registered nothing at all. Evidently he was attuned to both Falk and Orry—a rare feat in itself, in Falk's experience —for Orry was quite plainly listening as the telepathic speech began again.

"Men razed your mind and then taught you what they wished you to know—what they wish to believe. So taught, you distrust us. We feared it would be so. But ask what you will, Agad Ramarren of Werel; we will answer with the truth."

"How long have I been here?"

"Six days."

"Why was I drugged and befooled at first?"

"We were attempting to restore your memory. We failed."

Do not believe him, do not believe him, Falk told himself so urgently that no doubt the Shing, if he had any empathic skill at all, received the message clearly. That did not matter. The game must be played, and played their way, though they made all the rules and had all the skill. His ineptitude did not matter. His honesty did. He was staked now totally on one belief: that an honest man cannot be cheated, that truth, if the game be played through right to the end, will lead to truth.

"Tell me why I should trust you," he said.

The mindspeech, pure and clear as an electronically produced musical note, began again, while the sender Abundibot, and he and Orry, stood motionless as pieces on a chessboard.

"We whom you know as Shing are men. We are Terrans, born on Earth of human stock, as was your ancestor Jacob Agat of the First Colony on Werel. Men have taught you what they believe about the history of Earth in the twelve centuries since the Colony on Werel was founded. Now we—men also—will teach you what we know.

"No Enemy ever came from distant stars to attack the League of All Worlds. The League was destroyed by revolution, civil war, by its own corruption, militarism, despotism. On all the worlds there were revolts, rebellions, usurpations; from the Prime World came reprisals that scorched planets to black sand. No more lightspeed ships went out into so risky a future: only the FTLs, the missile-ships, the world-busters. Earth was not destroyed, but half its people were, its cities, its ships and ansibles, its records, its culture—all in two terrible years of civil war between the Loyalists and the Rebels, both armed with the unspeakable weapons developed by the League to fight an alien enemy.

"Some desperate men on Earth, dominating the struggle for a moment but knowing further counter-revolt and wreckage and ruin was inevitable, employed a new weapon. They lied. They invented a name for themselves, and a language, and some vague tales of the remote home-world they came from, and then they went spreading the rumor over Earth, in their own ranks and the Loyalist camps as well, that the Enemy had come. The civil war was all due to the Enemy. The Enemy had infiltrated everywhere, had wrecked the League and was running Earth, was in power now and was going to stop the war. And they had achieved all this by their one unexpectable, sinister, alien power: the power to mindlie.

"Men believed the tale. It suited their panic, their dismay, their weariness. Their world in ruins around them, they submitted to an Enemy whom they were glad to believe supernatural, invincible. They swallowed the bait of peace.

"And they have lived since then in peace.

"We of Es Toch tell a little myth, which says that in the beginning the Creator told a great lie. For there was nothing at all, but the Creator spoke, saying, It exists. And behold, in order that the lie of God might be God's truth, the universe at once began to exist. . . .

"If human peace depended on a lie, there were those willing to maintain the lie. Since men insisted that the Enemy had come and ruled the Earth, we called ourselves the Enemy, and ruled. None came to dispute our lie or wreck our peace; the worlds of the League are all sundered, the age of interstellar flight is past; once in a century, perhaps, some ship from a far world blunders here, like yours. There are rebels against our rule, such as those who attacked your ship at the Barrier. We try to control such rebels, for, rightly or wrongly, we beat and have borne for a millennium the burden of human peace. For having told a great lie, we must now uphold a great law. You know the law that we—men among men—enforce: the one Law, learned in humanity's most terrible hour."

The brilliant toneless mindspeech ceased; it was like the switching off of a light. In the silence like darkness which followed, young Orry whispered aloud, "Reverence for Life."

Silence again. Falk stood motionless, trying not to betray in his face or in his perhaps overheard thoughts the confusion and irresolution he felt. Was all he had learned false? Had mankind indeed no Enemy?

"If this history is the true one," he said at last, "why do you not tell it and prove it to men?"

"We are men," came the telepathic answer. "There are thousands upon thousands of us who know the truth. We are those who have power and knowledge, and use them for peace. There come dark ages, and this is one of them, all through man's history, when people will have it that the world is ruled by demons. We play the part of demons in their mythologies. When they begin to replace mythology with reason, we help them; and they learn the truth."

"Why do you tell me these things?"

"For truth's sake, and for your own."

"Who am I to deserve the truth?" Falk repeated coldly, looking across the room into Abundibot's masklike face.

"You were a messenger from a lost world, a colony of which all record was lost in the Years of Trouble. You came to Earth, and we, the Lords of Earth, failed to protect you. This is a shame and a grief to us. It was men of Earth who attacked you, killed or mindrazed all your company—men of Earth, of the planet to which, after so many centuries, you were returning. They were rebels

144

from Continent Three, which is neither so primitive nor so sparsely inhabited as this Continent One; they were using stolen interplanetary cars; they assumed that any lightspeed ship must belong to the 'Shing,' and so attacked it without warning. This we could have prevented, had we been more alert. We owe to you any reparation we can make."

"They have sought for you and the others all these years," Orry put in, earnest and a little pleading; obviously he very much wanted Falk to believe it all, to accept it, and to—to do what?

"You tried to restore my memory," Falk said. "Why?"

"Is that not what you came seeking here: your lost self?"

"Yes. It is. But I . . ." He did not even know what questions to ask; he could neither believe nor disbelieve all he had been told. There seemed to be no standard to judge it all by. That Zove and the others had lied to him was inconceivable, but that they themselves were deceived and ignorant was certainly possible. He was incredulous of everything Abundibot affirmed, and yet it had been mindsent, in clear immediate mindspeech where lying was impossible—or was it possible? If a liar says he is not lying—Falk gave it all up again. Looking once more at Abundibot he said, "Please do not bespeak me. I—I would rather hear your voice. You found, I think you said, that you could not restore my memory?"

Abundibot's muted, creaking whisper in Galaktika came strangely after the fluency of his sending. "Not by the means we used."

"By other means?"

"Possibly. We thought you had been given a parahypnotic block. Instead, you were mindrazed. We do not know where the rebels learned that technique, which we keep a close secret. An even closer secret is the fact that a razed mind can be restored." A smile appeared for a moment on the heavy, mask-like face, then disappeared completely. "With our psycho-computer techniques, we think we can effect the restoration in your case. However, this incurs the permanent total blocking of the replacement-personality; and this being so we did not wish to proceed without your consent."

The replacement-personality. . . . It meant nothing particular. What did it mean?

Falk felt a little cold creep over him, and he said carefully, "Do you mean that, in order to remember what I was, I must . . . forget what I am?"

"Unfortunately that is the case. We regret it very much. The loss, however, of a replacement-personality of a few years' growth is, though regrettable, perhaps not too high a price to pay for the repossession of a mind such as yours obviously was, and, of course, for the chance of completing your great mission across the stars and returning at last to your home with the knowledge you so gallantly came to seek."

Despite his rusty, unused-sounding whisper, Abundibot was as fluent in speaking as in mindspeaking; his words poured out and Falk caught the meaning, if he caught it, only on the third or fourth bounce. . . . "The chance—of completing—?" he repeated, feeling a fool, and glancing at Orry as if for support. "You mean, you would send me—us—back to . . . this planet I am supposed to have come from?"

"We would consider it an honor and a beginning of the reparation due you to give you a lightspeed ship for the voyage home to Werel."

146

"Earth is my home," Falk said with sudden violence. Abundibot was silent. After a minute the boy spoke: "Werel is mine, prech Ramarren," he said wistfully. "And I can never go back to it without you."

"Why not?"

"I don't know where it is. I was a child. Our ship was destroyed, the course-computers and all were blown up when we were attacked. I can't recalculate the course!"

"But these people have lightspeed ships and course-computers! What do you mean? What star does Werel circle, that's all you need to know."

"But I don't know it."

"This is nonsense." Falk began, pushed by mounting incredulity into anger. Abundibot held up his hand in a curiously potent gesture. "Let the boy explain, Agad Ramarren," he whispered.

"Explain that he doesn't know the name of his planet's sun?"

"It's true, prech Ramarren," Orry said shakily, his face crimson. "If—if you were only yourself, you'd know it without being told. I was in my ninth moonphase—I was still First Level. The Levels . . . Well, our civilization, at home, it's different from anything here, I guess. Now that I see it by the light of what the Lords here try to do, and democratic ideals, I realize it's very backward in some ways. But anyhow, there are the Levels, that cut across all the Orders and ranks, and make up the Basic Harmony of—prechnoye. . . . I don't know how to say it in Galaktika. Knowledge, I guess. Anyway I was on the First Level, being a child, and you were Eighth Level and Order. And each Level has—things you don't learn, and things you aren't told, and can't be told or understand, until you enter into it. And below the Seventh

Level, I think, you don't learn the True Name of the World or the True Name of the Sun—they're just the world, Werel, and the sun, prahan. The True Names are the old ones—they're in the Eighth Analect of the Books of Alterra, the books of the Colony. They're in Galaktika, so that they'd mean something to the Lords here. But I couldn't tell them, because I didn't know; all I know is 'sun' and 'world,' and that wouldn't get me home—nor you, if you can't remember what you knew! Which sun? Which world? Oh, you've got to let them give you your memory back, prech Ramarren! Do you see?"

"As through a glass," Falk said, "darkly."

And with the words from the Yaweh Canon he remembered all at once, certain and vivid amidst his bewilderment, the sun shining above the Clearing, bright on the windy, branch-embowered balconies of the Forest House. Then it was not his name he had come here to learn, but the sun's, the true name of the sun.

VIII

THE STRANGE UNSEEN Council of the Lords of Earth was over. In parting Abundibot had said to Falk, "The choice is yours: to remain Falk, our guest on Earth, or to regain your heritage and complete your destiny as Agad Ramar-ren of Werel. We wish that your choice be made know-ingly and in your own time. We await your decision and will abide by it." Then to Orry: "Make your kinsman free of the City, Har Orry, and let all he and you desire be known to us." The slit-door opened behind Abundibot and he withdrew, his tall bulky figure vanishing so abruptly outside the doorway that it seemed to have been flicked off. Had he in fact been there in substance, or only as some kind of projection? Falk was not sure. He wondered if he had yet seen a Shing or only the shadows and images of the Shing.

"Is there anywhere we can walk—out of doors?" he asked the boy abruptly, sick of the indirect and insub-stantial ways and walls of this place, and also wondering how far their freedom actually extended.

"Anywhere, prech Ramarren. Out in the streets—or shall we take a slider? Or there is a garden here in the Palace."

"A garden will do."

Orry led him down a great, empty, glowing corridor and through a valve-door into a small room. "The Garden," he said aloud, and the valve shut; there was no sense of motion but when it opened they stepped out into a garden. It was scarcely out of doors: the translucent walls glimmered with the lights of the City, far below; the moon, near full, shone hazy and distorted through the glassy roof. The place was full of soft moving lights and shadows, crowded with tropical shrubs and vines that twined about trellises and hung from arbors, their masses of cream and crimson flowers sweetening the steamy air, their leafage closing off vision within a few feet on every side. Falk turned suddenly to make sure that the path to the exit still lay clear behind him. The hot, heavy, perfumed silence was uncanny; it seemed to him for a moment that the ambiguous depths of the garden held a hint of something alien and enormously remote, the hues, the mood, the complexity of a lost world, a planet of perfumes and illusions, of swamps and transformations. . . .

On the path among the shadowy flowers Orry paused to take a small white tube from a case and insert it endwise between his lips, sucking on it eagerly. Falk was too absorbed in other impressions to pay much heed, but as if slightly embarrassed the boy explained, "It's pariitha, a tranquillant—the Lords all use it; it has a very stimulating effect on the mind. If you'd care to—"

"No, thanks. There are some more things I want to ask you." He hesitated, however. His new questions could not be entirely direct. Throughout the "Council" and

Abundibot's explanations he had felt, recurrently and uncomfortably, that the whole thing was a performance—a *play*, such as he had seen on ancient telescrolls in the library of the Prince of Kansas, the Dreamplay of Hain, the mad old king Lir raving on a stormswept heath. But the curious thing was his distinct impression that the play was not being acted for his benefit, but for Orry's. He did not understand why, but again and again he had felt that all Abundibot said to him was said to prove something to the boy.

And the boy believed it. It was no play to him; or else he was an actor in it.

"One thing puzzles me," Falk said, cautiously. "You told me that Werel is a hundred and thirty or forty light-years from Earth. There cannot be very many stars at just that distance.

"The Lords say there are four stars with planets that might be our system, between a hundred and fifteen and a hundred and fifty light-years away. But they are in four different directions, and if the Shing sent out a ship to search it could spend up to thirteen hundred years real-time going to and among those four to find the right one."

"Though you were a child, it seems a little strange that you didn't know how long the voyage was to take—how old you would be when you got home, as it were."

"It was spoken of as 'two years', prech Ramarren—that is, roughly a hundred and twenty Earth years—but it was clear to me that that was not the exact figure, and that I was not to ask the exact figure." For a moment, harking back thus to Werel, the boy spoke with a touch of sober resoluteness that he did not show at other times. "I think that perhaps, not knowing who or what they were going to find on Earth, the adults of the Expedition wanted to be sure that we children, with no mindguard technique, could not give away Werel's location to an enemy. It was safest for us to be ignorant, perhaps."

"Do you remember how the stars looked from Werel—the constellations?"

Orry shrugged for no, and smiled. "The Lords asked that too. I was Winter-born, prech Ramarren. Spring was just beginning when we left. I scarcely ever saw a cloudless sky."

If all this was true, then it would seem that in fact only he—his suppressed self, Ramarren—could say where he and Orry came from. Would that then explain what seemed almost the central puzzle, the interest the Shing took in him, their bringing him here under Estrel's tutelage, their offer to restore his memory? There was a world not under their control; it had re-invented light-speed flight; they would want to know where it was. And if they restored his memory, he could tell them. If they could restore his memory. If anything at all of what they had told him was true.

He sighed. He was weary of this turmoil of suspicions, this plethora of unsubstantiated marvels. At moments he wondered if he was still under the influence of some drug. He felt wholly inadequate to judge what he should do. He, and probably this boy, were like toys in the hands of strange faithless players.

"Was he—the one called Abundibot—was he in the room just now, or was it a projection, an illusion?"

"I don't know, prech Ramarren," Orry replied. The stuff he was breathing in from the tube seemed to cheer and soothe him; always rather childlike, he spoke now with blithe ease. "I expect he was there. But they never come close. I tell you—this is strange—in this long time I've been here, six years, I have never touched one of them. They keep very much apart, each one alone. I don't mean that they are unkind," he added hastily, looking with his clear eyes at Falk to make sure he had not given the wrong impression. "They are very kind. I am very fond of Lord Abundibot, and Ken Kenyek, and Parla. But they are so far—beyond me— They know so much. They bear so much. They keep knowledge alive, and keep the peace, and bear the burdens, and so they have done for a thousand years, while the rest of the people of Earth take no responsibility and live in brutish freedom. Their fellow men hate them and will not learn the truth they offer. And so they must always hold themselves apart, stay alone, in order to preserve the peace and the skills and knowledge that would be lost, without them, in a few years, among these warrior tribes and Houses and Wanderers and roving cannibals."

"They are not all cannibals," Falk said dryly.

Orry's well-learnt lesson seemed to have run out. "No," he agreed, "I suppose not."

"Some of them say that they have sunk so low because the Shing keep them low; that if they seek knowledge the Shing prevent them, if they seek to form a City of their own the Shing destroy it, and them."

There was a pause. Orry finished sucking on his tube of pariitha and carefully buried it around the roots of a shrub with long, hanging, flesh-red flowers. Falk waited for his answer and only gradually realized that there was not going to be one. What he had said simply had not penetrated, had not made sense to the boy.

They walked on a little among the shifting lights and damp fragrances of the garden, the moon blurred above them.

"The one whose image appeared first, just now . . . do you know her?"

"Strella Siobelbel," the boy answered readily. "Yes, I have seen her at Council Meetings before."

"Is she a Shing?"

"No, she's not one of the Lords; I think her people are mountain natives, but she was brought up in Es Toch. Many people bring or send their children here to be brought up in the service of the Lords. And children with subnormal minds are brought here and keyed into the psychocomputers, so that even they can share in the great work. Those are the ones the ignorant call toolmen. You came here with Strella Siobelbel, prech Ramarren?"

"Came with her; walked with her, ate with her, slept with her. She called herself Estrel, a Wanderer."

"You could have known she was not a Shing—" the boy said, then went red, and got out another of his tranquillant-tubes and began sucking on it.

"A Shing would not have slept with me?" Falk inquired. The boy shrugged his Werelian "No," still blushing; the drug finally encouraged him to speak and he said, "They do not touch common men, prech Ramarren—they are like gods, cold and kind and wise—they hold themselves apart—"

He was fluent, incoherent, childish. Did he know his own loneliness, orphaned and alien, living out his childhood and entering adolescence among these people who held themselves apart, who would not touch him, who stuffed him with words but left him so empty of reality that, at fifteen, he sought contentment from a drug? He certainly did not know·his isolation as such—he did not seem to have clear ideas on anything much—but it looked from his eyes sometimes, yearning, at Falk. Yearning and feebly hoping, the look of one perishing of thirst in a dry salt desert who looks up at a mirage. There was much more Falk wanted to ask him, but little use in asking. Pitying him, Falk put his hand on Orry's slender shoulder. The boy started at the touch, smiled timidly and vaguely, and sucked again at his tranquillant.

Back in his room, where everything was so luxuriously arranged for his comfort—and to impress Orry?— Falk paced a while like a caged bear, and finally lay down to sleep. In his dreams he was in a house, like the Forest House, but the people in the dream house had eyes the color of agate and amber. He tried to tell them he was one of them, their own kinsman, but they did not understand his speech and watched him strangely while he stammered and sought for the right words, the true words, the true name.

Toolmen waited to serve him when he woke. He dismissed them, and they left. He went out into the hall. No one barred his way; he met no one as he went on. It all seemed deserted, no one stirring in the long misty corridors or on the ramps or inside the half-seen, dim-walled rooms whose doors he could not find. Yet all the time he felt he was being watched, that every move he made was seen.

When he found his way back to his room Orry was waiting for him, wanting to show him about the city. All afternoon they explored, on foot and on a paristolis slider, the streets and terraced gardens, the bridges and palaces and dwellings of Es Toch. Orry was liberally provided with the slips of iridium that served as money, and when Falk remarked that he did not like the fancy-dress his hosts had provided him, Orry insisted they go to a clothier's shop and outfit him as he wished. He stood among racks and tables of gorgeous cloth, woven and plastiformed, dazzling with bright patterned colors; he thought of Parth weaving at her small loom in the sunlight, a pattern of white cranes on gray. "I will weave black cloth to wear," she had said, and remembering that he chose, from all the lovely rainbow of robes and gowns and clothing, black breeches and dark shirt and a short black cloak of wintercloth.

"Those are a little like our clothes at home—on Werel," Orry said, looking doubtfully for a moment at his own flame-red tunic. "Only we had no wintercloth there. Oh, there would be so much we could take back from Earth to Werel, to tell them and teach them, if we could go!"

They went on to an eating-place built out on a transparent shelf over the gorge. As the cold, bright evening of the high mountains darkened the abyss under them, the buildings that sprang up from its edges glowed iridescent and the streets and hanging bridges blazed with lights. Music undulated in the air about them as they ate the spice-disguised foods and watched the crowds of the city come and go.

Some of the people who walked in Es Toch were dressed poorly, some lavishly, many in the transvestite, gaudy apparel that Falk vaguely remembered seeing Estrel wear. There were many physical types, some different from any Falk had ever seen. One group was whitish-skinned, with blue eyes and hair like straw. Falk thought they had bleached themselves somehow, but Orry explained they were tribesmen from an area on Continent two, whose culture was being encouraged by the Shing,

156

who brought their leaders and young people here by air-car to see Es Toch and learn its ways. "You see, prech Ramarren, it is not true that the Lords refuse to teach the natives—it is the natives who refuse to learn. These white ones are sharing the Lords' knowledge."

"And what have they forgotten, to earn that prize?" Falk asked, but the question meant nothing to Orry. He knew almost nothing of any of the "natives," how they lived or what they knew. Shopkeepers and waiters he treated with condescension, pleasantly, as a man among inferiors. This arrogance he might have brought from Werel; he described Kelshak society as hierarchic, in-tensely conscious of each person's place on a scale or in an order, though what established the order, what values it was founded on, Falk did not understand. It was not mere birth-ranking, but Orry's childish memories did not suffice to give a clear picture. However that might be, Falk disliked the tone of the word "natives" in Orry's mouth, and he finally asked with a trace of irony, "How do you know which you should bow to and which should bow to you? I can't tell Lords from Natives. The Lords *are* natives—aren't they?"

"Oh, yes. The natives call themselves that, because they insist the Lords are alien conquerors. I can't always tell them apart either," the boy said with his vague, en-gaging, ingenuous smile.

"Most of these people in the streets are Shing?"

"I suppose so. Of course I only know a few by sight."

"I don't understand what keeps the Lords, the Shing, apart from the natives, if they are all Terran men to-gether."

"Why, knowledge, power—the Lords have been ruling

Earth for longer than the achinowao have been ruling Kelshy!"

"But they keep themselves a caste apart? You said the Lords believe in democracy." It was an antique word and had struck him when Orry used it; he was not sure of its meaning but knew it had to do with general participation in government.

"Yes, certainly, prech Ramarren. The Council rules democratically for the good of all, and there is no king or dictator. Shall we go to a pariitha-hall? They have stimulants, if you don't care for pariitha, and dancers and tëanb-players—"

"Do you like music?"

"No," the boy said with apologetic candor. "It makes me want to weep or scream. Of course on Werel only animals and little children sing. It is—it seems wrong to hear grown men do it. But the Lords like to encourage the native arts. And the dancing, sometimes that's very pretty . . ."

"No." A restlessness was rising strong in Falk, a will to see the thing through and be done with it. "I have a question for that one called Abundibot, if he will see us."

"Surely. He was my teacher for a long time; I can call him with this." Orry raised toward his mouth the gold-link bracelet on his wrist. While he spoke into it Falk sat remembering Estrel's muttered prayers to her amulet and marveling at his own vast obtuseness. Any fool might have guessed the thing was a transmitter; any fool but this one. . . . "Lord Abundibot says to come as soon as we please. He is in the East Palace," Orry announced, and they left, Orry tossing a slip of money to the bowing waiter who saw them out.

Spring thunderclouds had hidden stars and moon, but the streets blazed with light. Falk went through them with a heavy heart. Despite all his fears he had longed to see the city, *elonaae*, the Place of Men: but it only worried and wearied him. It was not the crowds that bothered him, though he had never in his memory seen more than ten houses or a hundred people together. It was not the reality of the city that was overwhelming, but its unreality. This was not a Place of Men. Es Toch gave no sense of history, of reaching back in time and out in space, though it had ruled the world for a millennium. There were none of the libraries, schools, museums which ancient telescrolls in Zove's House had led him to look for; there were no monuments or reminders of the Great Age of Man; there was no flow of learning or of goods. The money used was a mere largesse of the Shing, for there was no economy to give the place a true vitality of its own. Though there were said to be so many of the Lords, yet on Earth they kept only this one city, held apart, as Earth itself was held apart from the other worlds that once had formed the League. Es Toch was self-contained, self-nourished, rootless; all its brilliance and transcience of lights and machines and faces, its multiplicity of strangers, its luxurious complexity was built across a chasm in the ground, a hollow place. It was the Place of the Lie. Yet it was wonderful, like a carved jewel fallen in the vast wilderness of the Earth: wonderful, timeless, alien.

Their slider bore them over one of the swooping railless bridges towards a luminous tower. The river far below ran invisible in darkness; the mountains were hidden by night and storm and the city's glare. Toolmen met Falk and Orry at the entrance to the tower, ushered them into a valve-elevator and thence into a room whose walls, windowless and translucent as always, seemed made of bluish, sparkling mist. They were asked to be seated, and were served tall silver cups of some drink. Falk tasted it gingerly and was surprised to find it the same juniper-flavored liquor he had once been given in the Enclave of Kansas. He knew it was a strong intoxicant and drank no more; but Orry swigged his down with relish. Abundibot entered, tall, white-robed, mask-faced, dismissing the toolmen with a slight gesture. He stopped as some distance from Falk and Orry. The toolmen had left a third silver cup on the little stand. He raised it as if in salute, drank it right off, and then said in his dry whispering voice, "You do not drink, Lord Ramarren. There is an old, old saying on Earth: In wine is truth." He smiled and ceased smiling. "But your thirst is for the truth, not for the wine, perhaps."

"There is a question I wish to ask you."

"Only one?" The note of mockery seemed clear to Falk, so clear that he glanced at Orry to see if he had caught it. But the boy, sucking on another tube of pariitha, his gray-gold eyes lowered, had caught nothing.

"I should prefer to speak to you alone, for a moment," Falk said abruptly.

At that Orry looked up, puzzled; the Shing said, "You may, of course. It will make no difference, however, to my answer, if Har Orry is here or not here. There is nothing we keep from him that we might tell you, as there is nothing we might tell him and keep from you. If you prefer that he leave, however, it shall be so."

"Wait for me in the hall, Orry," Falk said; docile, the boy went out. When the vertical lips of the door had closed behind him, Falk said—whispered, rather, because everyone whispered here— "I wished to repeat what I asked you before. I am not sure I understood. You can restore my earlier memory only at the cost of my present memory—is that true?"

"Why do you ask me what is true? Will you believe it?"

"Why—why should I not believe it?" Falk replied, but his heart sank, for he felt the Shing was playing with him, as with a creature totally incompetent and powerless.

"Are we not the Liars? You must not believe anything we say. That is what you were taught in Zove's House, that is what you think. We know what you think."

"Tell me what I ask," Falk said, knowing the futility of his stubbornness.

"I will tell you what I told you before, and as best I can, though it is Ken Kenyek who knows these matters best. He is our most skilled mindhandler. Do you wish me to call him?—no doubt he will be willing to project to us here. No? It does not matter, of course. Crudely expressed, the answer to your question is this: Your mind was, as we say, razed. Mindrazing is an operation, not a surgical one of course, but a paramental one involving psychoelectric equipment, the effects of which are much more absolute than those of any mere hypnotic block. The restoration of a razed mind is possible, but is a much more drastic matter, accordingly, than the removal of a hypnotic block. What is in question, to you, at this moment, is a secondary, super-added, partial memory and personality-structure, which you now call your 'self.' This is, of course, not the case. Looked at impartially, this second-growth self of yours is a mere rudiment, emotionally stunted and intellectually incompetent, compared to the true self which lies so deeply hidden. As we cannot and do not expect you to be able to look at it impartially, however, we wish we could assure you that the restoration of Ramarren will include the continuity of Falk. And we have been tempted to lie to you about this, to spare you fear and doubt and make your decision easy. But it is best that you know the truth; we would not have it otherwise, nor, I think, would you. The truth is this: when we restore to its normal condition and function the synaptic totality of your original mind, if I may so simplify the incredibly complex operation which Ken Kenyek and his psychocomputers are ready to perform, this restoration will entail the total blocking of the secondary synaptic totality which you now consider to be your mind and self. This secondary totality will be irrecoverably suppressed: razed in its turn."

"To revive Ramarren you must kill Falk, then."

"We do not kill," the Shing said in his harsh whisper, then repeated it with blazing intensity in mindspeech—*"We do not kill!"*

There was a pause.

"To gain the great you must give up the less. It is always the rule," the Shing whispered.

"To live one must agree to die," Falk said, and saw the mask-face wince. "Very well. I agree. I consent to let you kill me. My consent does not really matter, does it?—yet you want it."

"We will not kill you." The whisper was louder. "We do not kill. We do not take life. We are restoring you to your true life and being. Only you must forget. That is the price; there is not any choice or doubt: to be Ramarren you must forget Falk. To this you must consent, indeed, but it is all we ask."

"Give me one day more," Falk said, and then rose, ending the conversation. He had lost; he was powerless. And yet he had made the mask wince, he had touched, for a moment, the very quick of the lie; and in that moment he had sensed that, had he the wits or strength to reach it, the truth lay very close at hand.

Falk left the building with Orry, and when they were in the street he said, "Come with me a minute. I want to speak with you outside those walls." They crossed the bright street to the edge of the cliff and stood side by side there in the cold night-wind of spring, the lights of the bridge shooting on out past them, over the black chasm that dropped sheer away from the street's edge.

"When I was Ramarren," Falk said slowly, "had I the right to ask a service of you?"

"Any service," the boy answered with the sober promptness that seemed to hark back to his early training on Werel.

Falk looked straight at him, holding his gaze a moment. He pointed to the bracelet of gold links on Orry's wrist, and with a gesture indicated that he should slip it off and toss it into the gorge.

Orry began to speak: Falk put his finger to his lips.

The boy's gaze flickered; he hesitated, then slipped the chain off and cast it down into the dark. Then he turned again to Falk his face in which fear, confusion, and the longing for approval were clear to see.

For the first time, Falk bespoke him in mindspeech: "Do you wear any other device or ornament, Orry?"

At first the boy did not understand. Falk's sending was inept and weak compared to that of the Shing. When he did at last understand, he replied paraverbally, with great clarity, "No, only the communicator. Why did you bid me throw it away?"

"I wish to speak with no listener but you, Orry."

The boy looked awed and scared. "The Lords can hear," he whispered aloud. "They can hear mindspeech anywhere, prech Ramarren—and I had only begun my training in mindguarding—"

"Then we'll speak aloud," Falk said, though he doubted that the Shing could overhear mindspeech "anywhere," without mechanical aid of some kind. "This is what I wish to ask you. These Lords of Es Toch brought me here, it seems, to restore my memory as Ramarren. But they can do it, or will do it, only at the cost of my memory of myself as I am now, and all I have learned on Earth. This they insist upon. I do not wish it to be so. I do not wish to forget what I know and guess, and be an ignorant tool in their hands. I do not wish to die again before my death! I don't think I can withstand them, but I will try, and the service I ask of you is this—" He stopped, hesitant among choices, for he had not worked out his plan at all.

Orry's face, which had been excited, now dulled with confusion again, and finally he said, "But why . . ."

"Well?" Falk said, seeing the authority he had briefly exerted over the boy evaporate. Still, he had shocked Orry into asking "Why?" and if he was ever to get through to the boy, it would be right now.

"Why do you mistrust the Lords? Why should they want to suppress your memory of Earth?"

"Because Ramarren does not know what I know. Nor do you. And our ignorance may betray the world that sent us here."

"But you . . . you don't even remember our world . . ."

"No. But I will not serve the Liars who rule this one. Listen to me. This is all I can guess of what they want. They will restore my former mind in order to learn the true name, the location of our home world. If they **learn** it while they are working on my mind, then I think they'll kill me then and there, and tell you that the operation was fatal; or raze my mind once more and tell you that the operation was a failure. If not, they'll let me live, at least until I tell them what they want to know. And I won't know enough, as Ramarren, not to tell them. Then they'll send us back to Werel—sole survivors of the great journey, returning after centuries to tell Werel how, on dark barbaric Earth, the Shing bravely hold the torch of civilization alight. The Shing who are no man's Enemy, the self-sacrificing Lords, the wise Lords who are really men of Earth, not aliens or conquerors. We will tell Werel all about the friendly Shing. And they'll believe us. They will believe the lies we believe. And so they will fear no attack from the Shing; and they will not send help to the men of Earth, the true men who await deliverance from the lie."

"But prech Ramarren, those are not lies," Orry said.

Falk looked at him a minute in the diffuse, bright, shifting light. His heart sank, but he said finally, "Will you do the service I asked of you?"

"Yes," the boy whispered.

"Without telling any other living being what it is?"

"Yes."

"It is simply this. When you first see me as Ramarren— if you ever do—then say to me these words: Read the first page of the book."

" 'Read the first page of the book,' " Orry repeated, docile.

There was a pause. Falk stood feeling himself encompassed by futility, like a fly bundled in spider-silk.

"Is that all the service, prech Ramarren?"

"That's all."

The boy bowed his head and muttered a sentence in his native tongue, evidently some formula of promising. Then he asked, "What should I tell them about the bracelet communicator, prech Ramarren?"

"The truth—it doesn't matter, if you keep the other secret," Falk said. It seemed, at least, that they had not taught the boy to lie. But they had not taught him to know truth from lies.

Orry took him back across the bridge on his slider, and he re-entered the shining, mist-walled palace where Estrel had first brought him. Once alone in his room he gave way to fear and rage, knowing how he was utterly fooled and made helpless; and when he had controlled his anger still he walked the room like a bear in a cage, contending with the fear of death.

If he besought them, might they not let him live on as Falk, who was useless to them, but harmless?

No. They would not. That was clear, and only cowardice made him turn to the notion. There was no hope there.

Could he escape?

Maybe. The seeming emptiness of this great building might be a sham, or a trap, or like so much else here, an illusion. He felt and guessed that he was constantly spied upon, aurally or visually, by hidden presences or devices. All doors were guarded by toolmen or electronic monitors. But if he did escape from Es Toch, what then?

Could he make his way back across the mountains, across the plains, through the forest, and come at last to

166

the Clearing, where Parth . . . No! He stopped himself in anger. He could not go back. This far he had come following his way, and he must follow on to the end: through death if it must be, to rebirth—the rebirth of a stranger, of an alien soul.

But there was no one here to tell that stranger and alien the truth. There was no one here that Falk could trust, except himself, and therefore not only must Falk die, but his dying must serve the will of the Enemy. That was what he could not bear; that was unendurable. He paced up and down the still, greenish dusk of his room. Blurred inaudible lightning flashed across the ceiling. He would not serve the Liars; he would not tell them what they wanted to know. It was not Werel he cared for—for all he knew, his guesses were all astray and Werel itself was a lie, Orry a more elaborate Estrel; there was no telling. But he loved Earth, though he was alien upon it. And Earth to him meant the house in the Forest, the sunlight on the Clearing, Parth. These he would not betray. He must believe that there was a way to keep himself, against all force and trickery, from betraying them.

Again and again he tried to imagine some way in which he as Falk could leave a message for himself as Ramarren: a problem in itself so grotesque it beggared his imagination, and beyond that, insoluble. If the Shing did not watch him write such a message, certainly they would find it when it was written. He had thought at first to use Orry as the go-between, ordering him to tell Ramarren, "Do not answer the Shing's questions," but he had not been able to trust Orry to obey, or to keep the order secret. The Shing had so mindhandled the boy that he was by now, essentially, their instrument; and even the meaningless message that Falk had given him might already be known to his Lords.

There was no device or trick, no means or way to get around or get out. There was only one hope, and that very small: that he could hold on; that through whatever they did to him he could keep hold of himself and refuse to forget, refuse to die. The only thing that gave him grounds for hoping that this might be possible was that the Shing had said it was impossible.

They wanted him to believe that it was impossible.

The delusions and apparitions and hallucinations of his first hours or days in Es Toch had been worked on him, then, only to confuse him and weaken his self-trust: for that was what they were after. They wanted him to distrust himself, his beliefs, his knowledge, his strength. All the explanations about mind-razing were then equally a scare, a bogey, to convince him that he could not possibly withstand their parahypnotic operations.

Ramarren had not withstood them. . . .

But Ramarren had had no suspicion or warning of their powers or what they would try to do to him, whereas Falk did. That might make a difference. Even so, Ramarren's memory had not been destroyed beyond recall, as they insisted Falk's would be: the proof of that was that they intended to recall it.

A hope; a very small hope. All he could do was say *I will survive* in the hope it might be true; and with luck, it would be. And without luck . . .?

Hope is a slighter, tougher thing even than trust, he thought, pacing his room as the soundless, vague lightning flashed overhead. In a good season one trusts life; in a bad season one only hopes. But they are of the same essence: they are the mind's indispensable relationship with other minds, with the world, and with time. Without trust, a man lives, but not a human life; without hope, he dies. When there is no relationship, where hands do not touch, emotion atrophies in void and intelligence goes sterile and obsessed. Between men the only link left is that of owner to slave, or murderer to victim.

Laws are made against the impulse a people most fears in itself. *Do not kill* was the Shing's vaunted single Law. All else was permitted: which meant, perhaps, there was little else they really wanted to do. . . . Fearing their own profound attraction towards death, they preached Reverence for Life, fooling themselves at last with their own lie.

Against them he could never prevail except, perhaps, through the one quality no liar can cope with, integrity. Perhaps it would not occur to them that a man could so will to be himself, to live his life, that he might resist them even when helpless in their hands.

Perhaps, perhaps.

Deliberately stilling his thoughts at last, he took up the book that the Prince of Kansas had given him and which, belying the Prince's prediction, he had not yet lost again, and read in it for a while, very intently, before he slept.

Next morning—his last, perhaps, of this life—Orry suggested that they sightsee by aircar, and Falk assented, saying that he wished to see the Western Ocean. With elaborate courtesy two of the Shing, Abundibot and Ken Kenyek, asked if they might accompany their honored guest, and answer any further questions he might wish to ask about the Dominion of Earth, or about the operation planned for tomorrow. Falk had had some vague hopes in fact of learning more details of what they planned to do to his mind, so as to be able to put up a stronger resistance to it. It was no good. Ken Kenyek poured out endless verbiage concerning neurons and synapses, salvaging, blocking, releasing, drugs, hypnosis, parahypnosis, brain-linked computers . . . none of which was meaningful, all of which was frightening. Falk soon ceased to try to understand.

The aircar, piloted by a speechless toolman who seemed little more than an extension of the controls, cleared the mountains and shot west over the deserts, bright with the brief flower of their spring. Within a few minutes they were nearing the granite face of the Western Range. Still sheered and smashed and raw from the cataclysms of two thousand years ago, the Sierras stood, jagged pinnacles upthrust from chasms of snow. Over the crests lay the ocean, bright in the sunlight; dark beneath the waves lay the drowned lands.

There were cities there, obliterated—as there were in his own mind forgotten cities, lost places, lost names. As the aircar circled to return eastward he said, "Tomorrow the earthquake; and Falk goes under. . . ."

"A pity it must be so, Lord Ramarren," Abundibot said with satisfaction. Or it seemed to Falk that he spoke with satisfaction. Whenever Abundibot expressed any emotion in words, the expression rang so false that it seemed to imply an opposite emotion; but perhaps what it implied actually was a total lack of any affect or feeling whatsoever. Ken Kenyek, white-faced and pale-eyed, with regular, ageless features, neither showed nor pretended any emotion when he spoke or when, as now, he sat motionless and expressionless, neither serene nor stolid but utterly closed, self-sufficient, remote.

The aircar flashed back across the desert miles between Es Toch and the sea; there was no sign of human habitation in all that great expanse. They landed on the roof of the building in which Falk's room was. After a couple of hours spent in the cold, heavy presence of the Shing he craved even that illusory solitude. They permitted him to have it; the rest of the afternoon and the evening he spent alone in the mist-walled room. He had feared the Shing might drug him again or send illusions to distract and weaken him, but apparently they felt they need take no more precautions with him. He was left undisturbed, to pace the translucent floor, to sit still, and to read in his book. What, after all, could he do against their will?

Again and again through the long hours he returned to the book, the Old Canon. He did not dare mark it even with his fingernail; he only read it, well as he knew it, with total absorption, page after page, yielding himself to the words, repeating them to himself as he paced or sat or lay, and returning again and again and yet again to the beginning, the first words of the first page:

> *The way that can be gone*
> *is not the eternal Way.*
> *The name that can be named*
> *is not the eternal Name.*

And far into the night, under the pressure of weariness and of hunger, of the thoughts he would not allow himself to think and the terror of death that he would not allow himself to feel, his mind entered at last the state he had sought. The walls fell away; his self fell away from him, and he was nothing. He was the words: he was the word, the word spoken in darkness with none to hear at the beginning, the first page of time. His self had fallen from him and he was utterly, everlastingly himself: nameless, single, one.

Gradually the moment returned, and things had names, and the walls arose. He read the first page of the book once again, and then lay down and slept.

The east wall of his room was emerald-bright with early sunlight when a couple of toolmen came for him and took him down through the misty hall and levels of the building to the street, and by slider through the shadowy streets and across the chasm to another tower. These two were not the servants who had waited on him, but a pair of big, speechless guards. Remembering the methodical brutality of the beating he had got when he had first entered Es Toch, the first lesson in self-distrust the Shing had given him, he guessed that they had been afraid he might try to escape at this last minute, and had provided these guards to discourage any such impulse.

He was taken into a maze of rooms that ended in brightly lit, underground cubicles all walled in by and dominated by the screens and banks of an immense computer complex. In one of these Ken Kenyek came forward to meet him, alone. It was curious how he had seen the Shing only one or two at a time, and very few of them in all. But there was no time to puzzle over that now, though on the fringes of his mind a vague memory, an explanation, danced for a moment, until Ken Kenyek spoke.

"You did not try to commit suicide last night," the Shing said in his toneless whisper.

That was in fact the one way out that had never occurred to Falk.

"I thought I would let you handle that," he said. .

Ken Kenyek paid no heed to his words, though he had an air of listening closely. "Everything is set up," he said. "These are the same banks and precisely the same connections which were used to block your primary mental-paramental structure six years ago. The removal of the block should be without difficulty or trauma, given your consent. Consent is essential to restoration, though not to repression. Are you ready now?" Almost simultaneously with his spoken words he bespoke Falk in that dazzlingly clear mindspeech: "Are you ready?"

He listened closely as Falk answered in kind, "I am."

As if satisfied by the answer or its empathic overtones, the Shing nodded once and said in his monotonous whisper, "I shall start out then without drugs. Drugs befog the clarity of the parahypnotic processes; it is easier to work without them. Sit down there."

Falk obeyed, silent, trying to keep his mind silent as well.

An assistant entered at some unspoken signal, and came over to Falk while Ken Kenyek sat down in front of one of the computer-banks, as a musician sits down to an instrument. For a moment Falk remembered the great patterning-frame in the Throneroom of Kansas, the swift dark hands that had hovered over it, forming and un-forming the certain, changeful patterns of stones, stars, thoughts. . . . A blackness came down like a curtain over his eyes and over his mind. He was aware that something was being fitted over his head, a hood or cap; then he was aware of nothing, only blackness, infinite blackness, the dark. In the dark a voice was speaking a word in his mind, a word he almost understood. Over and over the same word, the word, the word, the name . . . Like the flaring up of a light his will to survive flared up, and he declared it with terrible effort, against all odds, in silence: *I am Falk!*

Then darkness.

IX

This was a quiet place, and dim, like a deep forest. Weak, he lay a long time between sleep and waking. Often he dreamed or remembered fragments of a dream from earlier, deeper sleep. Then again he slept, and woke again to the dim verdant light and the quietness.

There was a movement near him. Turning his head, he saw a young man, a stranger.

"Who are you?"

"Har Orry."

The name dropped like a stone into the dreamy tranquillity of his mind and vanished. Only the circles from it widened out and widened out softly, slowly, until at last the outermost circle touched shore, and broke. Orry, Har Weden's son, one of the Voyagers . . . a boy, a child, winterborn.

The still surface of the pool of sleep was crisscrossed with a little disturbance. He closed his eyes again and willed to go under.

"I dreamed," he murmured with his eyes closed. "I had a lot of dreams. . . ."

But he was awake again, and looking into that frightened, irresolute, boyish face. It was Orry, Wedens son: Orry as he would look five or six moonphases from now, if they survived the Voyage.

What was it he had forgotten?

"What is this place?"

"Please lie still, prech Ramarren—don't talk yet; please lie still."

"What happened to me?" Dizziness forced him to obey the boy and lie back. His body, even the muscles of his lips and tongue as he spoke, did not obey him properly. It was not weakness but a queer lack of control. To raise his hand he had to use conscious volition, as if it were someone else's hand he was picking up.

Someone else's hand. . . . He stared at his arm and hand for a good while. The skin was curiously darkened to the color of tanned hann-hide. Down the forearm to the wrist ran a series of parallel bluish scars, slightly stippled, as if made by repeated jabs of a needle. Even the skin of the palm was toughened and weathered as if he had been out in the open for a long time, instead of in the laboratories and computer-rooms of Voyage Center and the Halls of Council and Places of Silence in Wegest. . . .

He looked around suddenly. The room he was in was windowless; but, weirdly, he could see the sunlight in and through its greenish walls.

"There was an accident," he said at last. "In the launching, or when . . . But we made the Voyage. We made it. Did I dream it?"

"No, prech Ramarren. We made the Voyage."

Silence again. He said after a while, "I can only remember the Voyage as if it were one night, one long night, last night. . . . But it aged you from a child almost to a man. We were wrong about that, then."

"No—the Voyage did not age me—" Orry stopped.

"Where are the others?"

"Lost."

"Dead? Speak entirely, vesprech Orry."

"Probably dead, prech Ramarren."

"What is this place?"

"Please, rest now—"

"Answer."

"This is a room in a city called Es Toch on the planet Earth," the boy answered with due entirety, and then broke out in a kind of wail, "You don't know it?—you don't remember it, any of it? This is worse than before—"

"How should J remember Earth?" Ramarren whispered.

"I—I was to say to you, *Read the first page of the book.*"

Ramarren paid no need to the boy's stammering. He knew now that all had gone amiss, and that a time had passed that he knew nothing of. But until he could master this strange weakness of his body he could do nothing, and so he was quiet until all dizziness had passed. Then with closed mind he told over certain of the Fifth Level Soliloquies; and when they had quieted his mind as well, he summoned sleep.

The dreams rose up about him once more, complex and frightening yet shot through with sweetness like the sunlight breaking through the dark of an old forest. With deeper sleep these fantasies dispersed, and his dream became a simple, vivid memory: He was waiting beside the airfoil to accompany his father to the city. Up on the foothills of Charn the forests were half leafless in their long dying, but the air was warm and clear and still. His father Agad Karsen, a lithe spare old man in his ceremonial garb and helmet, holding his office-stone, came leisurely across the lawn with his daughter, and both were laughing as he teased her about her first suitor, "Look out for that lad, Parth, he'll woo without mercy if you let him." Words lightly spoken long ago, in the sunlight of the long, golden autumn of his youth, he heard them again now, and the girl's laugh in response. Sister, little sister, beloved Arnan. . . . What had his father called her?—not by her right name but something else, another name—

Ramarren woke. He sat up, with a definite effort taking command of his body—yes, his, still hesitant and shaky but certainly his own. For a moment in waking he had felt he was a ghost in alien flesh, displaced, lost.

He was all right. He was Agad Ramarren, born in the silverstone house among broad lawns under the white peak of Charn, the Single Mountain; Agad's heir, fallborn, so that all his life had been lived in autumn and winter. Spring he had never seen, might never see, for the ship *Alterra* had begun her Voyage to Earth on the first day of spring. But the long winter and the fall, the length of his manhood, boyhood, childhood stretched back behind him vivid and unbroken, remembered, the river reaching upward to the source.

The boy Orry was no longer in the room. "Orry!" he said aloud; for he was able and determined now to learn what had happened to him, to his companions, to the *Alterra* and its mission. There was no reply or signal. The room seemed to be not only windowless but doorless. He checked his impulse to mindcall the boy; he did not know whether Orry was still tuned with him, and also since his own mind had evidently suffered either damage or interference, he had better go carefully and keep out of phase with any other mind, until he learned if he was threatened by volitional control or antichrony.

He stood up, dismissing vertigo and a brief, sharp occipital pain, and walked back and forth across the room a few times, getting himself into muscular harmony while he studied the outlandish clothes he was wearing and the queer room he was in. There was a lot of furniture, bed, tables, and sitting-places, all set up on long thin legs. The translucent, murky green walls were covered with explicitly deceptive and disjunctive patterns, one of which disguised an iris-door, another a half-length mirror. He stopped and looked at himself a moment. He looked thin, and weatherbeaten, and perhaps older; he hardly knew. He felt curiously self-conscious, looking at himself. What was this uneasiness, this lack of concentration? What had happened, what had been lost? He turned away and set himself to study the room again. There were various enigmatic objects about, and two of familiar type though foreign in detail: a drinking-cup on one table, and a leafed book beside it. He picked up the book. Something Orry had said flickered in his mind and went out again. The title was meaningless, though the characters were clearly related to the alphabet of the Tongue of the Books. He opened the thing and glanced through it. The left-hand pages were written—handwritten, it appeared—with columns of marvelously complicated patterns that might be holistic symbols, ideographs, technological shorthand. The right-hand pages were also handwritten, but in the letters that resembled the letters of the Books, Galaktika. A code-book? But he had not yet puzzled out more than a word or two when the doorslit silently irised open and a person entered the room: a woman.

Ramarren looked at her with intense curiosity, unguardedly and without fear; only perhaps, feeling himself vulnerable, he intensified a little the straight, authoritative gaze to which his birth, earned Level and arlesh entitled him. Unabashed, she returned his gaze. They stood there a moment in silence.

She was handsome and delicate, fantastically dressed, her hair bleached or reddish-pigmented. Her eyes were a dark circle set in a white oval. Eyes like the eyes of painted faces in the Lighall of the Old City, frescoes of dark-skinned, tall people building a town, warring with the Migrators, watching the stars: the Colonists, the Terrans of Alterra. . . .

Now Ramarren knew past doubt that he was indeed on Earth, that he had made his Voyage. He set pride and self-defense aside, and knelt down to her. To him, to all the people who had sent him on the mission across eight hundred and twenty-five trillion miles of nothingness, she was of a race that time and memory and forgetting had imbued with the quality of the divine. Single, individual as she stood before him, yet she was of the Race of Man and looked at him with the eyes of that Race, and he did honor to history and myth and the long exile of his ancestors, bowing his head to her as he knelt.

He rose and held out his open hands in the Kelshak gesture of reception, and she began to speak to him. Her speaking was strange, very strange, for though he had never seen her before her voice was infinitely familiar to his ear, and though he did not know the tongue she spoke he understood a word of it, then another. For a second this frightened him by its uncanniness and made him fear she was using some form of mindspeech that could penetrate even his outphase barrier; in the next second, he realized that he understood her because she was speaking the Tongue of the Books, Galaktika. Only her accent and her fluency in speaking it had kept him from recognizing it at once.

She had already said several sentences to him, speaking in a curiously cold, quick, lifeless way; ". . . not know I am here," she was saying. "Now tell me which of us is the liar, the faithless one. I walked with you all that endless way, I lay with you a hundred nights, and now you don't even know my name. Do you, Falk? Do you know my name? Do you know your own?"

"I am Agad Ramarren," he said, and his own name in his own voice sounded strange to him.

"Who told you so? You're Falk. Don't you know a man named Falk?—he used to wear your flesh. Ken Kenyek and Kradgy forbade me to say his name to you, but I'm sick of playing their games and never my own. I like to play my own games. Don't you remember your name, Falk?—Falk—Falk—don't you remember your name? Ah, you're still as stupid as you ever were, staring like a stranded fish!"

At once he dropped his gaze. The matter of looking directly into another person's eyes was a sensitive one among Werelians, and was strictly controlled by tabu and manners. That was his only response at first to her words, though his inward reactions were immediate and various. For one thing, she was lightly drugged, with something on the stimulant-hallucinogenic order: his trained perceptions reported this to him as a certainty, whether he liked its implications concerning the Race of Man or not. For another thing, he was not sure he had understood all she'd said and certainly had no idea what she was talking about, but her intent was aggressive, destructive. And the aggression was effective. For all his lack of comprehension, her weird jeers and the name she kept repeating moved and distressed him, shook him, shocked him.

He turned away a little to signify he would not cross her gaze again unless she wished, and said at last, softly, in the archaic tongue his people knew only from the ancient books of the Colony, "Are you of the Race of Man, or of the Enemy?"

She laughed in a forced, gibing way. "Both, Falk. There is no Enemy, and I work for them. Listen, tell Abundibot your name is Falk. Tell Ken Kenyek. Tell all the Lords your name is Falk—that'll give them something to worry about! Falk—"

"Enough."

His voice was as soft as before, but he had spoken with his full authority: she stopped with her mouth open, gaping. When she spoke again it was only to repeat that name she called him by, in a voice gone shaky and almost supplicating. She was pitiful, but he made no reply. She was in a temporary or permanent psychotic state, and he felt himself too vulnerable and too unsure, in these circumstances, to allow her further communication. He felt pretty shaky himself, and moving away from her he indrew, becoming only secondarily aware of her presence and voice. He needed to collect himself; there was something very strange the matter with him, not drugs, at least no drug he knew, but a profound displacement and imbalance, worse than any of the induced insanities of Seventh Level mental discipline. But he was given little time. The voice behind him rose in shrill rancor, and then he caught the shift to violence and along with it the sense of a second presence. He turned very quickly: she had begun to draw from her bizarre clothing what was obviously a weapon, but was standing frozen staring not at him but at a tall man in the doorway.

No word was spoken, but the newcomer directed at the woman a telepathic command of such shattering coercive force that it made Ramarren wince. The weapon dropped to the floor and the woman, making a thin keening sound, ran stooped from the room, trying to escape the destroying insistence of that mental order. Her blurred shadow wavered a moment in the wall, vanished.

The tall man turned his white-rimmed eyes to Ramarren and bespoke him with normal power: "Who are you?"

Ramarren answered in kind, "Agad Ramarren," but no more, nor did he bow. Things had gone even more wrong than he had first imagined. Who were these people? In the confrontation he had just witnessed there had been insanity, cruelty and terror, and nothing else; certainly nothing that disposed him either to reverence or trust.

But the tall man came forward a little, a smile on his heavy, rigid face, and spoke aloud courteously in the Tongue of the Books. "I am Pelleu Abundibot, and I welcome you heartily to Earth, kinsman, son of the long exile, messenger of the Lost Colony!"

Ramarren, at that, made a very brief bow and stood a moment in silence. "It appears," he said, "that I have been on Earth some while, and made an enemy of that woman, and earned certain scars. Will you tell me how this was, and how my shipmates perished? Bespeak me if you will: I do not speak Galaktika so well as you."

"Prech Ramarren," the other said—he had evidently

picked that up from Orry as if it were a mere honorific, and had no notion of what constituted the relationship of prechnoye—"forgive me first that I speak aloud. It is not our custom to use mindspeech except in urgent need, or to our inferiors. And forgive next the intrusion of that creature, a servant whose madness has driven her outside the Law. We will attend to her mind. She will not trouble you again. As for your questions, all will be answered. In brief, however, here is the unhappy tale which now at last draws to a happy ending. Your ship *Alterra* was attacked as it entered Earthspace by our enemies, rebels outside the Law. They took two or more of you off the *Alterra* into their small planetary cars before our guardship came. When it came, they destroyed the *Alterra* with all left aboard her, and scattered in their small ships. We caught the one on which Har Orry was prisoner, but you were carried off—I do not know for what purpose. They did not kill you, but erased your memory back to the pre-lingual stage, and then turned you loose in a wild forest to find your death. You survived, and were given shelter by barbarians of the forest; finally our searchers found you, brought you here, and by parahypnotic techniques we have succeeded in restoring your memory. It was all we could do—little indeed, but all."

Ramarren listened intently. The story shook him, and he made no effort to hide his feelings; but he felt also a certain uneasiness or suspicion, which he did conceal. The tall man had addressed him, though very briefly, in mindspeech, and thus given him a degree of attunement. Then Abundibot had ceased all telepathic sending and had put up an empathic guard, but not a perfect one; Ramarren, highly sensitive and finely trained, received vague empathic impressions so much at discrepancy with

184

what the man said as to hint at dementia, or at lying. Or was he himself so out of tune with himself—as he might well be after parahypnosis—that his empathic receptions were simply not reliable?

"How long . . .?" he asked at last, looking up for a moment into those alien eyes.

"Six years ago Terran style, prech Ramarren."

The Terran year was nearly the length of a moonphase. "So long," he said. He could not take it in. His friends, his fellow-Voyagers had been dead then for a long time, and he had been alone on Earth . . . "Six years?"

"You remember nothing of those years?"

"Nothing."

"We were forced to wipe out what rudimentary memory you may have had of that time, in order to restore your true memory and personality. We very much regret that loss of six years of your life. But they would not have been sane or pleasant memories. The outlaw brutes had made of you a creature more brutish than themselves. I am glad you do not remember it, prech Ramarren."

Not only glad, but gleeful. This man must have very little empathic ability or training, or he would be putting up a better guard; his telepathic guard was flawless. More and more distracted by these mindheard overtones that implied falsity or unclarity in what Abundibot said, and by the continuing lack of coherence in his own mind, even in his physical reactions, which remained slow and uncertain, Ramarren had to pull himself together to make any response at all. Memories—how could six years have passed without his remembering one moment from them? But a hundred and forty years had passed while his light-speed ship had crossed from Werel to Earth and of that he remembered only a moment, indeed, one terrible, eternal moment. . . . What had the madwoman called him, screaming a name at him with crazy, grieving rancor?

"What was I called, these past six years?"

"Called? Among the natives, do you mean, prech Ramarren? I am not sure what name they gave you, if they bothered to give you any. . . ."

Falk, she had called him, Falk. "Fellowman," he said abruptly, translating the Kelshak form of address into Galaktika, "I will learn more of you later, if you will. What you tell me troubles me. Let me be alone with it a while."

"Surely, surely, prech Ramarren. Your young friend Orry is eager to be with you—shall I send him to you?" But Ramarren, having made his request and heard it accepted, had in the way of one of his Level dismissed the other, tuned him out, hearing whatever else he said simply as noise.

"We too have much to learn of you, and are eager to learn it, once you feel quite recovered." Silence. Then the noise again: "Our servants wait to serve you; if you desire refreshment or company you have only to go to the door and speak." Silence again, and at last the unmannerly presence withdrew.

Ramarren sent no speculations after it. He was too preoccupied with himself to worry about these strange hosts of his. The turmoil within his mind was increasing sharply, coming to some kind of crisis. He felt as if he were being dragged to face something that he could not endure to face, and at the same time craved to face, to find. The bitterest days of his Seventh Level training had only been a hint of this disintegration of his emotions and identity, for that had been an induced psychosis, carefully controlled, and this was not under his control. Or was it?—was he leading himself into this, compelling himself towards the crisis? But who was "he" who compelled and was compelled? He had been killed, and brought back to life. What was death, then, the death he could not remember?

To escape the utter panic welling up in him he looked around for any object to fix on, reverting to early trance-discipline, the Outcome technique of fixing on one concrete thing to build up the world from once more. But everything about him was alien, deceptive, unfamiliar; the very floor under him was a dull sheet of mist. There was the book he had been looking at when the woman entered calling him by that name he would not remember. He would not remember it. The book: he had held it in his hands, it was real, it was there. He picked it up very carefully and stared at the page that it opened to. Columns of beautiful meaningless patterns, lines of half-comprehensible script, changed from the letters he had learned long ago in the First Analect, deviant, bewildering. He stared at them and could not read them, and a word of which he did not know the meaning rose up from them, the first word:

The way . . .

He looked from the book to his own hand that held it. Whose hand, darkened and scarred beneath an alien sun? Whose hand?

*The way that can be gone
is not the eternal Way.
The name. . .*

He could not remember the name; he would not read it. In a dream he had read these words, in a long sleep, a death, a dream.

> *The name that can be named*
> *is not the eternal Name.*

And with that the dream rose up overwhelming him like a wave rising, and broke.

He was Falk, and he was Ramarren. He was the fool and the wise man: one man twice born.

In those first fearful hours, he begged and prayed to be delivered sometimes from one self, sometimes from the other. Once when he cried out in anguish in his own native tongue, he did not understand the words he had spoken, and this was so terrible that in utter misery he wept; it was Falk who did not understand, but Ramarren who wept.

In that same moment of misery he touched for the first time, for a moment only, the balance-pole, the center, and for a moment was *himself*: then lost again, but with just enough strength to hope for the next moment of harmony. Harmony: when he was Ramarren he clung to that idea and discipline, and it was perhaps his mastery of that central Kelshak doctrine that kept him from going right over the edge into madness. But there was no integrating or balancing the two minds and personalities that shared his skull, not yet; he must swing between them, blanking one out for the other's sake, then drawn at once back the other way. He was scarcely able to move, being plagued by the hallucination of having two bodies, of being actually physically two different men.

He did not dare sleep, though he was worn out: he feared the waking too much.

It was night, and he was left to himself. *To myselves*, Falk commented. Falk was at first the stronger, having had some preparation for this ordeal. It was Falk who got the first dialogue going: *I have got to get some sleep, Ramarren,* he said, and Ramarren received the words as if in mindspeech and without premeditation replied in kind: *I'm afraid to sleep.* Then he kept watch for a little while, and knew Falk's dreams like shadows and echoes in his mind.

He got through this first, worst time, and by the time morning shone dim through the green veilwalls of his room, he had lost his fear and was beginning to gain real control over both thought and action.

There was of course no actual overlap of his two sets of memories. Falk had come to conscious being in the vast number of neurons that in a highly intelligent brain remain unused—the fallow fields of Ramarren's mind. The basic motor and sensory paths has never been blocked off and so in a sense had been shared all along, though difficulties arose there caused by the doubling of the sets of motor habits and modes of perception. An object looked different to him depending on whether he looked at it as Falk or as Ramarren, and though in the long run this reduplication might prove an augmentation of his intelligence and perceptive power, at the moment it was confusing to the point of vertigo. There was considerable emotional intershading, so that his feelings on some points quite literally conflicted. And, since Falk's memories covered his "lifetime" just as did Ramarren's, the two series tended to appear simultaneously instead of in proper sequence. It was hard for Ramarren to allow for the gap of time during which he had not consciously existed. Ten days ago where had he been? He had been on muleback among the snowy mountains of Earth; Falk knew that; but Ramarren knew that he had been taking leave of his wife in a house on the high green plains of Werel . . . . Also, what Ramarren guessed about Terra was often contradicted by what Falk knew, while Falk's ignorance of Werel cast a strange glamor of legend over Ramarren's own past. Yet even in this bewilderment there was the germ of interaction, of the coherence toward which he strove. For the fact remained, he was, bodily and chronologically, one man: his problem was not really that of creating a unity, only of comprehending it.

Coherence was far from being gained. One or the other of the two memory-structures still had to dominate, if he was to think and act with any competence. Most often, now, it was Ramarren who took over, for the Navigator of the *Alterra* was a decisive and potent person. Falk, in comparison, felt himself childish, tentative; he could offer what knowledge he had, but relied upon Ramarren's strength and experience. Both were needed, for the two-minded man was in a very obscure and hazardous situation.

One question was basic to all the others. It was simply put: whether or not the Shing could be trusted. For if Falk had merely been inculcated with a groundless fear of the Lords of Earth, then the hazards and obscurities would themselves prove groundless. At first Ramarren thought this might well be the case; but he did not think it for long.

There were open lies and discrepancies which already his double memory had caught. Abundibot had refused to mindspeak to Ramarren, saying the Shing avoided paraverbal communication: that Falk knew to be a lie. Why had Abundibot told it? Evidently because he wanted to tell a lie—the Shing story of what had happened to the *Alterra* and its crew—and could not or dared not tell it to Ramarren in mindspeech.

But he had told Falk very much the same story, in mindspeech.

If it was a false story, then, the Shing could and did mindlie. Was it false?

Ramarren called upon Falk's memory. At first that effort of combination was beyond him, but it became easier as he struggled, pacing up and down the silent room, and suddenly it came clear; he could recall the brilliant silence of Abundibot's words: "We whom you know as Shing are men. . . ." And hearing it even in memory, Ramarren knew it for a lie. It was incredible, and indubitable. The Shing could lie telepathically—that guess and dread of subjected humanity was right. The Shing were, in truth, the Enemy.

They were not men but aliens, gifted with an alien power; and no doubt they had broken the League and gained power over Earth by the use of that power. And it was they who had attacked the *Alterra* as she had come into Earthspace; all the talk of rebels was mere fiction. They had killed or brainrazed all the crew but the child Orry. Ramarren could guess why: because they had discovered, testing him or one of the other highly trained paraverbalists of the crew, that a Werelian could tell when they were mindlying. That had frightened the Shing, and they had done away with the adults, saving out only the harmless child as an informant.

To Ramarren it was only yesterday that his fellow-

Voyagers had perished, and, struggling against that blow, he tried to think that like him they might have survived somewhere on Earth. But if they had—and he had been very lucky—where were they now? The Shing had had a hard time locating even one, it appeared, when they had discovered that they needed him.

What did they need him for? Why had they sought him, brought him here, restored the memory that they had destroyed?

No explanation could be got from the facts at his disposal except the one he had arrived at as Falk: The Shing needed him to tell them where he came from.

That gave Falk-Ramarren his first amount of amusement. If it really was that simple, it was funny. They had saved out Orry because he was so young; untrained, unformed, vulnerable, amenable, a perfect instrument and informant. He certainly had been all of that. But did not know where he came from. . . . And by the time they discovered that, they had wiped the information they wanted clean out of the minds that knew it, and scattered their victims over the wild, ruined Earth to die of accident or starvation or the attack of wild beasts or men.

He could assume that Ken Kenyek, while manipulating his mind through the psychocomputer yesterday, had tried to get him to divulge the Galaktika name of Werel's sun. And he could assume that if he had divulged it, he would be dead or mindless now. They did not want him, Ramarren; they wanted only his knowledge. And they had not got it.

That in itself must have them worried, and well it might. The Kelshak code of secrecy concerning the Books of the Lost Colony had evolved along with a whole technique of mindguarding. That mystique of secrecy—or more precisely of restraint—had grown over the long years from the rigorous control of scientific-technical knowledge exercised by the original Colonists, itself an outgrowth from the League's Law of Cultural Embargo, which forbade cultural importation to colonial planets. The whole concept of restraint was fundamental in Werelian culture by now, and the stratification of Werelian society was directed by the conviction that knowledge and technique must remain under intelligent control. Such details as the True Name of the Sun were formal and symbolical, but the formalism was taken seriously—with ultimate seriousness, for in Kelshy knowledge was religion, religion knowledge. To guard the intangible holy places in the minds of men, intangible and invulnerable defenses had been devised. Unless he was in one of the Places of Silence, and addressed in a certain form by an associate of his own Level, Ramarren was absolutely unable to communicate, in words or writing or mindspeech, the True Name of his world's sun.

He possessed, of course, equivalent knowledge: the complex of astronomical facts that had enabled him to plot the *Alterra*'s coordinates from Werel to Earth; his knowledge of the exact distance between the two planets' suns; his clear, astronomer's memory of the stars as seen from Werel. They had not got this information from him yet, probably because his mind had been in too chaotic a state when first restored by Ken Kenyek's manipulations, or because even then his parahypnotically strengthened mindguards and specific barriers had been functioning. Knowing there might still be an Enemy on Earth, the crewmen of the *Alterra* had not set off unprepared. Unless Shing mindscience was much stronger than Werelian, they would not now be able to force him to tell them

193

anything. They hoped to induce him, to persuade him. Therefore, for the present, he was at least physically safe.

—So long as they did not know that he remembered his existence as Falk.

That came over him with a chill. It had not occurred to him before. As Falk he had been useless to them, but harmless. As Ramarren he was useful to them, and harmless. But as Falk-Ramarren, he was a threat. And they did not tolerate threats: they could not afford to.

And there was the answer to the last question: Why did they want so badly to know where Werel was—what did Werel matter to them?

Again Falk's memory spoke to Ramarren's intelligence, this time recalling a calm, blithe, ironic voice. The old Listener in the deep forest spoke, the old man lonelier on Earth than even Falk had been: "There are not very many of the Shing. . . ."

A great piece of news and wisdom and advice, he had called it; and it must be the literal truth. The old histories Falk had learned in Zove's House held the Shing to be aliens from a very distant region of the galaxy, out beyond the Hyades, a matter perhaps of thousands of light-years. If that was so, probably no vast numbers of them had crossed so immense a length of spacetime. There had been enough to infiltrate the League and break it, given their powers of mindlying and other skills or weapons they might possess or have possessed; but had there been enough of them to rule over all the worlds they had divided and conquered? Planets were very large places, on any scale but that of the spaces in between them. The Shing must have had to spread themselves thin, and take much care to keep the subject planets from re-allying and joining to rebel. Orry had told Falk that the Shing did not seem to travel or trade much by lightspeed; he had never even seen a lightspeed ship of theirs. Was that because they feared their own kin on other worlds, grown away from them over the centuries of their dominion? Or conceivably was Earth the only planet they still ruled, defending it from all explorations from other worlds? No telling; but it did seem likely that on Earth there were indeed not very many of them.

They had refused to believe Orry's tale of how the Terrans on Werel had mutated toward the local biological norm and so finally blended stocks with the native hominids. They had said that was impossible: which meant that it had not happened to them; they were unable to mate with Terrans. They were still alien, then, after twelve hundred years; still isolated on Earth. And did they in fact rule mankind, from this single City? Once again Ramarren turned to Falk for the answer, and saw it as No. They controlled men by habit, ruse, fear, and weaponry, by being quick to prevent the rise of any strong tribe or the pooling of knowledge that might threaten them. They prevented men from doing anything. But they did nothing themselves. They did not rule, they only blighted.

It was clear, then, why Werel posed a deadly threat to them. They had so far kept up their tenuous, ruinous hold on the culture which long ago they had wrecked and redirected; but a strong, numerous, technologically advanced race, with a mythos of blood-kinship with the Terrans, and a mindscience and weaponry equal to their own, might crush them at a blow. And deliver men from them.

If they learned from him where Werel was, would they send out a lightspeed bomb-ship, like a long fuse burning across the light-years, to destroy the dangerous world before it ever learned of their existence?

That seemed only too possible. Yet two things told against it: their careful preparation of young Orry, as if they wanted him to act as a messenger; and their singular Law.

Falk-Ramarren was unable to decide whether that rule of Reverence for Life was the Shing's one genuine belief, their one plank across the abyss of self-destruction that underlay their behavior as the black canyon gaped beneath their city, or instead was simply the biggest lie of all their lies. They did in fact seem to avoid killing sentient beings. They had left him alive, and perhaps the others; their elaborately disguised foods were all vegetable; in order to control populations they evidently pitted tribe against tribe, starting the war but letting humans do the killing; and the histories told that in the early days of their rule, they had used eugenics and resettlement to consolidate their empire, rather than genocide. It might be true, then, that they obeyed their Law, in their own fashion.

In that case, their grooming of young Orry indicated that he was to be their messenger. Sole survivor of the Voyage, he was to return across the gulfs of time and space to Werel and tell them all the Shing had told him about Earth—quack, quack, like the birds that quacked *It is wrong to take life,* the moral boar, the squeaking mice in the foundations of the house of Man. . . . Mindless, honest, disastrous, Orry would carry the Lie to Werel.

Honor and the memory of the Colony were strong forces on Werel, and a call for help from Earth might bring help from them; but if they were told there was not and never had been an Enemy, that Earth was an ancient happy garden-spot, they were not likely to make that long journey just to see it. And if they did they would come unarmed, as Ramarren and his companions had come.

Another voice spoke in his memory, longer ago yet, deeper in the forest: "We cannot go on like this forever. There must be a hope, a sign. . . ."

He had not been sent with a message to mankind, as Zove had dreamed. The hope was a stranger one even than that, the sign more obscure. He was to carry mankind's message, to utter their cry for help, for deliverance. *I must go home; I must tell them the truth,* he thought, knowing that the Shing would at all costs prevent this, that Orry would be sent, and he would be kept here or killed.

In the great weariness of his long effort to think coherently, his will relaxed all at once, his chancy control over his racked and worried double mind broke. He dropped down exhausted on the couch and put his head in his hands. *If I could only go home,* he thought; *if I could walk once more with Parth down in the Long Field. . . .*

That was the dream-self grieving, the dreamer Falk. Ramarren tried to evade that hopeless yearning by thinking of his wife, dark-haired, golden-eyed, in a gown sewn with a thousand tiny chains of silver, his wife Adrise. But his wedding-ring was gone. And Adrise was dead. She had been dead a long, long time. She had married Ramarren knowing that they would have little more than a moonphase together, for he was going on the Voyage to Terra. And during that one, terrible moment of his Voyage, she had lived out her life, grown old, died;

197

she had been dead for a hundred of Earth's years, perhaps. Across the years between the stars, which now was the dreamer, which the dream?

"You should have died a century ago," the Prince of Kansas had told uncomprehending Falk, seeing or sensing or knowing of the man that lay lost within him, the man born so long ago. And now if Ramarren were to return to Werel it would be yet farther into his own future. Nearly three centuries, nearly five of Werel's great Years would then have elapsed since he had left; all would be changed; he would be as strange on Werel as he had been on Earth.

There was only one place to which he could truly go home, to the welcome of those who had loved him: Zove's House. And he would never see it again. If his way led anywhere, it was out, away from Earth. He was on his own, and had only one job to do: to try to follow that way through to the end.

X

It was broad daylight now, and realizing that he was very hungry Ramarren went to the concealed door and asked aloud, in Galaktika, for food. There was no reply, but presently a toolman brought and served him food; and as he was finishing it a little signal sounded outside the door. "Come in!" Ramarren said in Kelshak, and Har Orry entered, then the tall Shing Abundibot, and two others whom Ramarren had never seen. Yet their names were in his mind: Ken Kenyek and Kradgy. They were introduced to him; politenesses were uttered. Ramarren found that he could handle himself pretty well; the necessity of keeping Falk completely hidden and suppressed was actually a convenience, freeing him to behave spontaneously. He was aware that the mentalist Ken Kenyek was trying to mindprobe, and with considerable skill and force, but that did not worry him. If his barriers had held good even under the parahypnotic hood, they certainly would not falter now.

None of the Shing bespoke him. They stood about in their strange stiff fashion as if afraid of being touched, and whispered all they said. Ramarren managed to ask some of the questions which as Ramarren he might be expected to ask concerning Earth, mankind, the Shing, and listened gravely to the answers. Once he tried to get into phase with young Orry, but failed. The boy had no real guard up, but perhaps had been subjected to some mental treatment which nullified the little skill in phase-catching he had learned as a child, and also was under the influence of the drug he had been habituated to. Even as Ramarren sent him the slight, familiar signal of their relationship in prechnoye, Orry began sucking on a tube of pariitha. In the vivid distracting world of semi-hallucination it provided him, his perceptions were dulled, and he received nothing.

"You have seen nothing of Earth as yet but this one room," the one dressed as a woman, Kradgy, said to Ramarren in a harsh whisper. Ramarren was wary of them all, but Kradgy roused an instinctive fear or aversion in him; there was a hint of nightmare in the bulky body under flowing robes, the long purplish-black hair, the harsh, precise whisper.

"I should like to see more."

"We shall show you whatever you wish to see. The Earth is open to its honored visitor."

"I do not remember seeing Earth from the *Alterra* when we came into orbit," Ramarren said in stiff, Werelian-accented Galaktika. "Nor do I remember the attack on the ship. Can you tell me why this is so?"

The question might be risky, but he was genuinely curious for the answer; it was the one blank still left in his double memory.

"You were in the condition we term achronia," Ken Kenyek replied. "You came out of lightspeed all at once at the Barrier, since your ship had no retemporalizer. You were at that moment, and for some minutes or hours after, either unconscious or insane."

"We had not run into the problem in our short runs at lightspeed."

"The longer the flight, the stronger the Barrier."

"It was a gallant thing," Abundibot said in his creaky whisper and with his usual floridity, "a journey of a hundred and twenty-five light-years in a scarcely tested ship!"

Ramarren accepted the compliment without correcting the number.

"Come, my Lords, let us show our guest the City of Earth." Simultaneously with Abundibot's words, Ramarren caught the passage of mindspeech between Kradgy and Ken Kenyek, but did not get the sense of it; he was too intent on maintaining his own guard to be able to mindhear or even to receive much empathic impression.

"The ship in which you return to Werel," Ken Kenyek said, "will of course be furnished with a retemporalizer, and you will suffer no derangement at re-entering planetary space."

Ramarren had risen, rather awkwardly—Falk was used to chairs but Ramarren was not, and had felt most uncomfortable perched up in mid-air—but he stood still now and after a moment asked, "The ship in which we return—?"

Orry looked up with blurry hopefulness. Kradgy yawned, showing strong yellow teeth. Abundibot said, "When you have seen all you wish to see of Earth and have learned all you wish to learn, we have a lightspeed ship ready for you to go home to Werel in—you, Lord Agad, and Har Orry. We ourselves travel little. There are no more wars; we have no need for trade with other worlds; and we do not wish to bankrupt poor Earth again with the immense cost of lightspeed ships merely to assuage our curiosity. We Men of Earth are an old race now; we stay home, tend our garden, and do not meddle and explore abroad. But your Voyage must be completed, your mission fulfilled. The *New Alterra* awaits you at our spaceport, and Werel awaits your return. It is a great pity that your civilization had not rediscovered the ansible principle, so that we could be in communication with them now. By now, of course, they may have the instantaneous transmitter; but we cannot signal them, having no coordinates."

"Indeed," Ramarren said politely.

There was a slight, tense pause.

"I do not think I understand," he said.

"The ansible—"

"I understand what the ansible transmitter did, though not how it did it. As you say, sir, we had not when I left Werel rediscovered the principles of instantaneous transmission. But I do not understand what prevented you from attempting to signal Werel."

Dangerous ground. He was all alert now, in control, a player in the game not a piece to be moved: and he sensed the electric tension behind the three rigid faces.

"Prech Ramarren," Abundibot said, "as Har Orry was too young to have learned the precise distances involved, we have never had the honor of knowing exactly where Werel is located, though of course we have a general idea. As he had learned very little Galaktika, Har Orry was unable to tell us the Galaktika name for Werel's sun, which of course would be meaningful to us, who share the language with you as a heritage from the days of the

League. Therefore we have been forced to wait for your assistance, before we could attempt ansible contact with Werel, or prepare the coordinates on the ship we have ready for you."

"You do not know the name of the star Werel circles?"

"That unfortunately is the case. If you care to tell us—"

"I cannot tell you."

The Shing could not be surprised; they were too self-absorbed, too egocentric. Abundibot and Ken Kenyek registered nothing at all. Kradgy said in his strange, dreary, precise whisper, "You mean you don't know either?"

"I cannot tell you the True Name of the Sun," Ramarren said serenely.

This time he caught the flicker of mindspeech, Ken Kenyek to Abundibot: *I told you so.*

"I apologize, prech Ramarren for my ignorance in inquiring after a forbidden matter. Will you forgive me? We do not know your ways, and though ignorance is a poor excuse it is all I can plead." Abundibot was creaking on when all at once the boy Orry interrupted him, scared into wakefulness:

"Prech Ramarren, you—you will be able to set the ship's coordinates? You do remember what—what you knew as Navigator?"

Ramarren turned to him and asked quietly, "Do you want to go home, vesprechna?"

"Yes!"

"In twenty or thirty days, if it pleases these Lords who offer us so great a gift, we shall return in their ship to Werel. I am sorry," he went on, turning back to the Shing, "that my mouth and mind are closed to your question. My silence is a mean return for your generous frankness." Had they been using mindspeech, he thought, the exchange would have been a great deal less polite; for he, unlike the Shing, was unable to mindlie, and therefore probably could not have said one word of his last speech.

"No matter, Lord Agad! It is your safe return, not our questions, that is important! So long as you can program the ship—and all our records and course-computers are at your service when you may require them—then the question is as good as answered." And indeed it was, for if they wanted to know where Werel was they would only have to examine the course he programmed into their ship. After that, if they still distrusted him, they could re-erase his mind, explaining to Orry that the restoration of his memory had caused him finally to break down. They would then send Orry off to deliver their message to Werel. They did still distrust him, because they knew he could detect their mindlying. If there was any way out of the trap he had not found it yet.

They all went together through the misty halls, down the ramps and elevators, out of the palace into daylight. Falk's element of the double mind was almost entirely repressed now, and Ramarren moved and thought and spoke quite freely as Ramarren. He sensed the constant, sharp readiness of the Shing minds, particularly that of Ken Kenyek, waiting to penetrate the least flaw or catch the slightest slip. The very pressure kept him doubly alert. So it was as Ramarren, the alien, that he looked up into the sky of late morning and saw Earth's yellow sun.

He stopped, caught by sudden joy. For it was something, no matter what had gone before and what might follow after—it was something to have seen the light, in one lifetime, of two suns. The orange gold of Werel's sun, the white gold of Earth's: he could hold them now side by side as a man might hold two jewels, comparing their beauty for the sake of heightening their praise.

The boy was standing beside him; and Ramarren murmured aloud the greeting that Kelshak babies and little children were taught to say to the sun seen at dawn or after the long storms of winter, "Welcome the star of life, the center of the year . . ." Orry picked it up midway and spoke it with him. It was the first harmony between them, and Ramarren was glad of it, for he would need Orry before this game was done.

A slider was summoned and they went about the city, Ramarren asking appropriate questions and the Shing replying as they saw fit. Abundibot described elaborately how all of Es Toch, towers, bridges, streets and palaces, had been built overnight a thousand years ago, on a river-isle on the other side of the planet, and how from century to century whenever they felt inclined the Lords of Earth summoned their wondrous machines and instruments to move the whole city to a new site suiting their whim. It was a pretty tale; and Orry was too benumbed with drugs and persuasions to disbelieve anything, while if Ramarren believed or not was little matter. Abundibot evidently told lies for the mere pleasure of it. Perhaps it was the only pleasure he knew. There were elaborate descriptions also of how Earth was governed, how most of the Shing spent their lives among common men, disguised as mere "natives" but working for the master plan emanating from Es Toch, how carefree and content most of humanity was in their knowledge that the Shing would keep the peace and bear the burdens, how arts and learning were gently encouraged and rebellious and destructive elements as gently repressed. A planet of humble people, in their humble little cottages and peaceful tribes and town-

lets; no warring, no killing, no crowding; the old achieve-
ments and ambitions forgotten; almost a race of children,
protected by the firm kindly guidance and the invulnerable technological strength of the Shing caste. . . .

The story went on and on, always the same with varia-
tions, soothing and reassuring. It was no wonder the poor
waif Orry believed it; Ramarren would have believed
most of it, if he had not had Falk's memories of the
Forest and the Plains to show the rather subtle but total
falseness of it. Falk had not lived on Earth among children, but among men, brutalized, suffering, and impas-
sioned.

That day they showed Ramarren all over Es Toch,
which seemed to him who had lived among the old
streets of Wegest and in the great Winterhouses of Kas-
pool a sham city, vapid and artificial, impressive only by
its fantastic natural setting. Then they began to take him
and Orry about the world by aircar and planetary car, all-
day tours under the guidance of Abundibot or Ken Kenyek, jaunts to each of Earth's continents and even out to
the desolate and long-abandoned Moon. The days went
on; they went on playing the play for Orry's benefit,
wooing Ramarren till they got from him what they
wanted to know. Though he was directly or electronically
watched at every moment, visually and telepathically, he
was in no way restrained; evidently they felt they had
nothing to fear from him now.

Perhaps they would let him go home with Orry, then.
Perhaps they thought him harmless enough, in his ignorance, to be allowed to leave Earth with his readjusted
mind intact.

But he could buy his escape from Earth only with the
information they wanted, the location of Werel. So far he

had told them nothing and they had asked nothing more.

Did it so much matter, after all, if the Shing knew where Werel was?

It did. Though they might not be planning any immediate attack on this potential enemy, they might well be planning to send a robot monitor out after the *New Alterra*, with an ansible transmitter aboard to make instantaneous report to them of any preparation for interstellar flight on Werel. The ansible would give them a hundred and forty year start on the Werelians; they could stop an expedition to Terra before it started. The one advantage that Werel possessed tactically over the Shing was the fact that the Shing did not know where it was and might have to spend several centuries looking for it. Ramarren could buy a chance of escape only at the price of certain peril for the world to which he was responsible.

So he played for time, trying to devise a way out of his dilemma, flying with Orry and one or another of the Shing here and there over the Earth, which stretched out under their flight like a great lovely garden gone all to weeds and wilderness. He sought with all his trained intelligence some way in which he could turn his situation about and become the controller instead of the one controlled: for so his Kelshak mentality presented his case to him. Seen rightly, any situation, even a chaos or a trap would come clear and lead of itself to its one proper outcome: for there is in the long run no disharmony, only misunderstanding, no chance or mis-chance but only the ignorant eye. So Ramarren thought, and the second soul within him, Falk, took no issue with this view, but spent no time trying to think it all out, either. For Falk had seen the dull and bright stones slip across the wires of the patterning-frame, and had lived with men in their fallen estate, kings in exile on their own domain the Earth, and to him it seemed that no man could make his fate or control the game, but only wait for the bright jewel luck to slip by on the wire of time. Harmony exists, but there is no understanding it; the Way cannot be gone. So while Ramarren racked his mind, Falk lay low and waited. And when the chance came he caught it.

Or rather, as it turned out, he was caught by it.

There was nothing special about the moment. They were with Ken Kenyek in a fleet little auto-pilot aircar, one of the beautiful, clever machines that allowed the Shing to control and police the world so effectively. They were returning toward Es Toch from a long flight out over the islands of the Western Ocean, on one of which they had made a stop of several hours at a human settle-ment. The natives of the island-chain they had visited were handsome, contented people entirely absorbed in sailing, swimming, and sex—afloat in the azure amniotic sea: perfect specimens of human happiness and back-wardness to show the Werelians. Nothing to worry about there, nothing to fear.

Orry was dozing, with a pariitha-tube between his fin-gers. Ken Kenyek had put the ship on automatic, and with Ramarren—three or four feet away from him, as always, for the Shing never got physically close to any-one—was looking out the glass side of the aircar at the five-hundred-mile circle of fair weather and blue sea that surrounded them. Ramarren was tired, and let himself relax a little in this pleasant moment of suspension, aloft in a glass bubble in the center of the great blue and golden sphere.

"It is a lovely world," the Shing said.

"It is."

"The jewel of all worlds. . . . Is Werel as beautiful?"

"No. It is harsher."

"Yes, the long year would make it so. How long?— sixty Earthyears?"

"Yes."

"You were born in the fall, you said. That would mean you had never seen your world in summer when you left it."

"Once, when I flew to the Southern hemisphere. But their summers are cooler, as their winters are warmer, than in Kelshy. I have not seen the Great Summer of the north."

"You may yet. If you return within a few months, what will the season be on Werel?"

Ramarren computed for a couple of seconds and replied, "Late summer; about the twentieth moonphase of summer, perhaps."

"I made it to be fall—how long does the journey take?"

"A hundred and forty-two Earthyears," Ramarren said, and as he said it a little gust of panic blew across his mind and died away. He sensed the presence of the Shing's mind in his own; while talking, Ken Kenyek had reached out mentally, found his defenses down, and taken whole-phase control of his mind. That was all right. It showed incredible patience and telepathic skill on the Shing's part. He had been afraid of it, but now that it had happened it was perfectly all right.

Ken Kenyek was bespeaking him now, not in the creaky oral whisper of the Shing but in clear, comfortable mindspeech: "Now, that's all right, that's right, that's good. Isn't it pleasant that we're attuned at last?"

"Very pleasant," Ramarren agreed.

"Yes indeed. Now we can remain attuned and all our

worries are over. Well then, a hundred and forty-two lightyears distant—that means that your sun must be the one in the Dragon constellation. What is its name in Galaktika? No, that's right, you can't say it or bespeak it here. Eltanin, is that it, the name of your sun?"

Ramarren made no response of any kind.

"Eltanin, the Dragon's Eye, yes, that's very nice. The others we had picked as possibilities are somewhat closer in. Now this saves a great deal of time. We had almost—"

The quick, clear, mocking, soothing mindspeech stopped abruptly and Ken Kenyek gave a convulsive start; so did Ramarren at the identical moment. The Shing turned jerkily toward the controls of the aircar, then away. He leaned over in a strange fashion, too far over, like a puppet on strings carelessly managed, then all at once slid to the floor of the car and lay there with his white, handsome face upturned, rigid.

Orry, shaken from his euphoric drowse, was staring. "What's wrong? What happened?"

He got no answer. Ramarren was standing as rigidly as the Shing lay, and his eyes were locked with the Shing's in a double unseeing stare. When at last he moved, he spoke in a language Orry did not know. Then, laboriously, he spoke in Galaktika. "Put the ship in hover," he said.

The boy gaped. "What's wrong with Lord Ken, prech Ramarren?"

"Get up. Put the ship in hover!"

He was speaking Galaktika now not with his Werelian accent but in the debased form used by Earth natives. But though the language was wrong the urgency and authority were powerful. Orry obeyed him. The little glass bubble hung motionless in the center of the bowl of ocean, eastward of the sun.

"Prechna, is the—"

"Be still!"

Silence. Ken Kenyek lay still. Very gradually Ramarren's visible tension and intensity relaxed.

What had happened on the mental plane between him and Ken Kenyek was a matter of ambush and re-ambush. In physical terms, the Shing had jumped Ramarren, thinking he was capturing one man, and had in turn been surprised by a second man—the mind in ambush, Falk. Only for a second had Falk been able to take control and only by sheer force of surprise, but that had been long enough to free Ramarren from the Shing's phase-control. The instant he was free, while Ken Kenyek's mind was still in phase with his and vulnerable, Ramarren had taken control. It took all his skill and all his strength to keep Ken Kenyek's mind phased with his, helpless and assenting, as his own had been a moment before. But his advantage still remained: he was still double-minded, and while Ramarren held the Shing helpless, Falk was free to think and act.

This was the chance, the moment; there would be no other.

Falk asked aloud, "Where is there a lightspeed ship ready for flight?"

It was curious to hear the Shing answer in his whispering voice and know, for once to know certainly and absolutely, that he was not lying. "In the desert northwest of Es Toch."

"Is it guarded?"

"Yes."

"By live guards?"

"No."

"You will guide us there."

"I will guide you there."

"Take the car where he tells you, Orry."

"I don't understand, prech Ramarren; are we—"

"We are going to leave Earth. Now. Take the controls."

"Take the controls," Ken Kenyek repeated softly.

Orry obeyed, following the Shing's instructions as to course. At full speed the aircar shot eastward, yet seemed still to hang in the changeless center of the sea-sphere, towards the circumference of which the sun, behind them, dropped visibly. Then the Western Isles appeared, seeming to float towards them over the wrinkled glittering curve of the sea; then behind these the sharp white peaks of the coast appeared, and approached, and ran by beneath the aircar. Now they were over the dun desert broken by arid, fluted ranges casting long shadows to the east. Still following Ken Kenyek's murmured instructions, Orry slowed the ship, circled one of these ranges, set the controls to catch the landing-beacon and let the car be homed in. The high lifeless mountains rose up about them, walling them in, as the aircar settled down on a pale, shadowy plain.

No spaceport or airfield was visible, no roads, no buildings, but certain vague, very large shapes trembled mirage-like over the sand and sagebrush under the dark slopes of the mountains. Falk stared at them and could not focus his eyes on them, and it was Orry who said with a catch of his breath, "Starships."

They were the interstellar ships of the Shing, their fleet or part of it, camouflaged with light-dispeller nets. Those Falk had first seen were smaller ones; there were others, which he had taken for foothills. . . .

The aircar had intangibly settled itself down beside a

tiny, ruined, roofless shack, its boards bleached and split by the desert wind.

"What is that shack?"

"The entrance to the underground rooms is to one side of it."

"Are there ground-computers down there?"

"Yes."

"Are any of the small ships ready to go?"

"They are all ready to go. They are mostly robot-controlled defense ships."

"Is there one with pilot-control?"

"Yes. The one intended for Har Orry."

Ramarren kept close telepathic hold on the Shing's mind while Falk ordered him to take them to the ship and show them the onboard computers. Ken Kenyek at once obeyed. Falk-Ramarren had not entirely expected him to: there were limits to mind-control just as there were to normal hypnotic suggestion. The drive to self-preservation often resisted even the strongest control, and sometimes shattered the whole attunement when infringed upon. But the treason he was being forced to commit apparently aroused no instinctive resistance in Ken Kenyek; he took them into the starship and replied obediently to all Falk-Ramarren's questions, then led them back to the decrepit hut and at command unlocked, with physical and mental signals, the trapdoor in the sand near the door. They entered the tunnel that was revealed. At each of the underground doors and defenses and shields Ken Kenyek gave the proper signal or response, and so brought them at last to attack-proof, cataclysm-proof, thief-proof rooms far underground, where the automatic control guides and the course computers were.

Over an hour had now passed since the moment in the aircar. Ken Kenyek, assenting and submissive, reminding Falk at moments of poor Estrel, stood harmlessly by— harmless so long as Ramarren kept total control over his brain. The instant that control was relaxed, Ken Kenyek would send a mindcall to Es Toch if he had the power, or trip some alarm, and the other Shing and their toolmen would be here within a couple of minutes. But Ramarren must relax that control: for he needed his mind to think with. Falk did not know how to program a computer for the lightspeed course to Werel, satellite of the sun El-tanin. Only Ramarren could do that.

Falk had his own resources, however. "Give me your gun."

Ken Kenyek at once handed over a little weapon kept concealed under his elaborate robes. At this Orry stared in horror. Falk did not try to allay the boy's shock; in fact, he rubbed it in. "Reverence for Life?" he inquired coldly, examining the weapon. Actually, as he had expected, it was not a gun or laser but a lowlevel stunner without kill capacity. He turned it on Ken Kenyek, pitiful in his utter lack of resistance, and fired. At that Orry screamed and lunged forward, and Falk turned the stunner on him. Then he turned away from the two sprawled, paralyzed figures, his hands shaking, and let Ramarren take over as he pleased. He had done his share for the time being.

Ramarren had no time to spend on compunction or anxiety. He went straight to the computers and set to work. He already knew from his examination of the on-board controls that the mathematics involved in some of the ship's operations was not the familiar Cetian-based mathematics which Terrans still used and from which

Werel's mathematics, via the Colony, also derived. Some of the processes the Shing used and built into their computers were entirely alien to Cetian mathematical process and logic; and nothing else could have so firmly persuaded Ramarren that the Shing were, indeed, alien to Earth, alien to all the old League worlds, conquerors from some very distant world. He had never been quite sure that Earth's old histories and tales were correct on that point, but now he was convinced. He was, after all, essentially a mathematician.

It was just as well that he was, or certain of those processes would have stopped him cold in his effort to set up the coordinates for Werel on the Shing computers. As it was, the job took him five hours. All this time he had to keep, literally, half his mind on Ken Kenyek and Orry. It was simpler to keep Orry unconscious than to explain to him or order him about; it was absolutely vital that Ken Kenyek stay completely unconscious. Fortunately the stunner was an effective little device, and once he discovered the proper setting Falk only had to use it once more. Then he was free to coexist, as it were, while Ramarren plugged away at his computations.

Falk looked at nothing while Ramarren worked, but listened for any noise, and was conscious always of the two motionless, senseless figures sprawled out nearby. And he thought; he thought about Estrel, wondering where she was now and what she was now. Had they retrained her, razed her mind, killed her? No, they did not kill. They were afraid to kill and afraid to die, and called their fear Reverence for Life. The Shing, the Enemy, the Liars. . . . Did they in truth lie? Perhaps that was not quite the way of it; perhaps the essence of their lying was a profound, irremediable lack of understand-

ing. They could not get into touch with men. They had
used that and profited by it, making it into a great
weapon, the mindlie; but had it been worth their while,
after all? Twelve centuries of lying, ever since they had
first come here, exiles or pirates or empire-builders from
some distant star, determined to rule over these races
whose minds made no sense to them and whose flesh was
to them forever sterile. Alone, isolated, deafmutes ruling
deafmutes in a world of delusions. *Oh desolation. . . .*

Ramarren was done. After his five hours of driving
labor, and eight seconds of work for the computer, the
little iridium output slip was in his hand, ready to program into the ship's course-control.

He turned and stared foggily at Orry and Ken Kenyek.
What to do with them? They had to come along, evidently. *Erase the records on the computers,* said a voice
inside his mind, a familiar voice, his own—Falk's. Ramarren was dizzy with fatigue, but gradually he saw the
point of this request, and obeyed. Then he could not
think what to do next. And so, finally, for the first time,
he gave up, made no effort to dominate, let himself fuse
into . . . himself.

Falk-Ramarren got to work at once. He dragged Ken
Kenyek laboriously up to ground level and across the
starlit sand to the ship that trembled half-visible, opales-
cent in the desert night; he loaded the inert body into a
contourseat, gave it an extra dose of the stunner, and
then came back for Orry.

Orry began to revive partway, and managed to climb
feebly into the ship himself. "Prech Ramarren," he said
hoarsely, clutching at Falk-Ramarren's arm, "where are
we going?"

"To Werel."

216

"He's coming too—Ken Kenyek?"

"Yes. He can tell Werel his tale about Earth, and you can tell yours, and I mine. . . . There's always more than one way towards the truth. Strap yourself in. That's it."

Falk-Ramarren fed the little metal strip into the course-controller. It was accepted, and he set the ship to act within three minutes. With a last glance at the desert and the stars, he shut the ports and came hurridly, shaky with fatigue and strain, to strap himself in beside Orry and the Shing.

Lift-off was fusionpowered: the lightspeed drive would go into effect only at the outer edge of Earthspace. They took off very softly and were out of the atmosphere in a few seconds. The visual screens opened automatically, and Falk-Ramarren saw the Earth falling away, a great dusky bluish curve, bright-rimmed. Then the ship came out into the unending sunlight.

Was he leaving home, or going home?

On the screen dawn coming over the Eastern Ocean shone in a golden crescent for a moment against the dust of stars, like a jewel on a great patterning frame. Then frame and pattern shattered, the barrier was passed, and the little ship broke free of time and took them out across the darkness.

Ursula K. Le Guin

POUL ANDERSON